Saint Maybe

ANNE TYLER

Saint Maybe

ALFRED A. KNOPF

NEW YORK

1991

Contents

Saint Maybe

1

The Airmail Bowling Ball

On Waverly Street, everybody knew everybody else. It was only one short block, after all—a narrow strip of patched and repatched pavement, bracketed between a high stone cemetery wall at one end and the commercial clutter of Govans Road at the other. The trees were elderly maples with lumpy, bulbous trunks. The squat clapboard houses seemed mostly front porch.

And each house had its own particular role to play. Number Nine, for instance, was foreign. A constantly shifting assortment of Middle Eastern graduate students came and went, attending classes at Johns Hopkins, and the scent of exotic spices drifted from their kitchen every evening at suppertime. Number Six was referred to as the newlyweds', although the Crains had been married two years now and were beginning to look a bit worn around the edges. And Number Eight was the Bedloe family. They were never just the Bedloes, but the Bedloe *family*, Waverly Street's version of the ideal, apple-pie household: two amiable parents, three good-looking children, a dog, a cat, a scattering of goldfish.

In fact, the oldest of those children had long ago married and left—moved out to Baltimore County and started a family of her own—and the second-born was nearing thirty. But somehow the Bedloes were stuck in people's minds at a stage from a dozen years back, when Claudia was a college girl in bobby socks and Danny was captain of his high-school football team and Ian, the baby (his parents' big surprise), was still tearing down the sidewalk on his tricycle with a miniature license plate from a cereal box wired to the handlebar.

Now Ian was seventeen and, like the rest of his family, large-boned and handsome and easygoing, quick to make friends, fond of a good time. He had the Bedloe golden-brown hair, golden skin, and sleepy-looking brown eyes, although his mouth was his mother's, a pale beige mouth quirking upward at the corners. He liked to wear ragged jeans and plaid shirts—cotton broadcloth in summer, flannel in winter—unbuttoned all the way to expose a stretched-out T-shirt underneath. His shoes were high-top sneakers held together with electrical tape. This was in 1965, when Poe High School still maintained at least a vestige of a dress code, and his teachers were forever sending him home to put on something more presentable. (But his mother was likely to greet him in baggy, lint-covered slacks and one of his own shirts, her fading blond curls pinned scrappily back with a grand-daughter's pink plastic hairbow. *She* would not have passed the dress code either.) Also, there were complaints about the quality of Ian's schoolwork. He was bright, his teachers said, but lazy. Content to slide through with low B's or even C's. It was the spring of his junior year and if he didn't soon mend his ways, no self-respecting college would have him.

Ian listened to all this with a tolerant, bemused expression.

Things would turn out fine, he felt. Hadn't they always? (None of the Bedloes was a worrier.) Crowds of loyal friends had surrounded him since kindergarten. His sweetheart, Cicely Brown, was the prettiest girl in the junior class. His mother doted on him and his father—Poe's combination algebra teacher and baseball coach—let him pitch in nearly every game, and not just because they were related, either. His father claimed Ian had talent. In fact sometimes Ian daydreamed about pitching for the Orioles, but he knew he didn't have *that* much talent. He was a medium kind of guy, all in all.

Even so, there were moments when he believed that someday, somehow, he was going to end up famous. Famous for what, he couldn't quite say; but he'd be walking up the back steps or something and all at once he would imagine a camera zooming in on him, filming his life story. He imagined the level, cultured voice of his biographer saying, "Ian climbed the steps. He opened the door. He entered the kitchen."

"Have a good day, hon?" his mother asked, passing through with a laundry basket.

"Oh," he said, "the usual run of scholastic triumphs and athletic glories." And he set his books on the table.

His biographer said, "He set his books on the table."

That was the spring that Ian's brother fell in love. Up till then Danny had had his share of girlfriends—various decorative Peggies or Debbies to hang upon his arm—but somehow nothing had come of them. He was always getting dumped, it seemed, or sadly disillusioned. His mother had started fretting that he'd passed the point of no return and would wind up a seedy bachelor type. Now here was Lucy, slender and pretty and dressed in red, standing in the Bedloes' front hall with her back so straight, her purse held so firmly in both hands, that she seemed even smaller than she was. She seemed childlike, in fact, although Danny described her as a "woman" when he introduced her. "Mom,

Dad, Ian, I'd like you to meet the woman who's changed my life." Then Danny turned to Mrs. Jordan, who had chosen this inopportune moment to step across the street and borrow the pinking shears. "Mrs. Jordan: Lucy Dean."

His mother, skipping several stages of acquaintanceship, swept Lucy into a hug. (Clearly more was called for than a handshake.) His father said, "Well, now! What do you know!" The dog gave Lucy's crotch a friendly sniff, while Mrs. Jordan—an older lady, the soul of tact—hastily murmured something or other and backed out the door. And Ian clamped his palms in his armpits and grinned at no one in particular.

They moved to the living room, Ian bringing up the rear. Lucy perched in an easy chair and Danny settled on its arm, with one hand resting protectively behind her loose knot of black hair. To Ian, Lucy resembled some brightly feathered bird held captive by his brown plaid family. Her face was very small, a cameo face. Her dress was scoop-necked and slim-waisted and full-skirted. She wore extremely red lipstick that seemed not gaudy, for some reason, but brave. Ian was entranced.

"Tell us everything," Bee Bedloe ordered. "Where you met, how you got to know each other—everything."

She and Ian's father had seated themselves on the sofa. (Ian's father, who had a baseball player's mild, sloping build, was pulling in his stomach.) Ian himself remained slouched against the door frame.

"We met at the post office," Danny said. He beamed down at Lucy, who smiled back at him trustfully.

Bee said, "Oh? You two work together?"

"No, no," Lucy said, in a surprisingly croaky little drawl. "I went in to mail a package and Danny was the one who waited on me."

Danny told them, "She was mailing a package to Cheyenne, Wyoming, by air. I told her it would cost twenty dollars and twenty-seven cents. You could see it was more than she'd planned on—"

"I said, 'Twenty twenty-seven! Great God Almighty!' " Lucy squawked, startling everyone.

"So I told her, 'It's cheaper by parcel post, you know. That would be four sixty-three.' 'Let me think,' she says, and moves on out of the way. Gives up her place at the counter. Stands a few feet down from me, frowning at the wall."

"I had to take a minute to decide," Lucy explained.

"Frowns at the wall for the *longest* time. Three customers go ahead of her. Finally I say, 'Miss? You ready?' But she just goes on frowning."

"I was mailing some odds and ends to my ex-husband and I wanted to be shed of them as fast as possible," Lucy said.

A little jolt passed through the room.

Bee said, "Ex-husband?"

"Half of me wanted him to get that box tomorrow, even yesterday if it could be arranged, but the other half was counting pennies. 'That's fifteen-and-some dollars' difference,' this other half was saying. 'Think of all the groceries fifteen dollars could buy. Or shoes and stuff for the children.' "

"Children?"

"What got to me," Danny said, "was how she wouldn't be hurried. How it didn't bother her what other people made of her. I mean she just stood there pondering, little bit of a person. Then finally she said, 'Well,' and straightened her shoulders and chose to spring for airmail."

"It mattered just enough, I decided," Lucy said. "It was worth it just for the satisfaction."

"If she had said parcel post I might have let her go," Danny said. "But airmail! I admired that. I asked if she'd like to have dinner."

"He was the best-looking thing I'd seen in ages," Lucy told the Bedloes. "I said I'd be thrilled to have dinner."

Bee and Doug Bedloe sat side by side, smiling extra hard as if someone had just informed them that they were being photographed.

. . .

There was this about the Bedloes: They believed that every part of their lives was absolutely wonderful. It wasn't just an act, either. They really did believe it. Or at least Ian's mother did, and she was the one who set the tone. Her marriage was a great joy to her, her house made her happy every time she walked into it, and her children were attractive and kind and universally liked. When bad things happened—the usual accidents, illnesses, jogs in the established pattern—Bee treated them with eye-rolling good humor, as if they were the stuff of situation comedy. They would form new chapters in the lighthearted ongoing saga she entertained the neighbors with: How Claudia Totaled the Car. How Ian Got Suspended from First Grade.

As for Ian, he believed it too but only after a kind of hitch, a moment of hesitation. For instance, from time to time he had the feeling that his father was something of a joke at Poe High— ineffectual at discipline, and muddled in his explanation of the more complicated algebraic functions. But Bee said he was the most popular teacher Poe had ever employed, and in fact that was true. Yes, certainly it was true. Ian knew she was right.

Or look at Claudia. The family's one scholar, she had dropped out of college her senior year to get married, and then the babies started coming so thick and so fast that they had to be named alphabetically: Abbie, Barney, Cindy, Davey . . . Where would it all end? some cynical voice inquired from the depths of Ian's mind. Xavier? Zelda? But his mother said she hoped they would progress to *double* letters—Aaron Abel and Bonnie Belinda—like items on a crowded catalog page. Then Ian saw Claudia's children as a tumbling hodgepodge heaped in a basket, and he was forced to smile.

Or Danny. Wasn't it sort of a comedown that Danny had gone to work at the post office straight out of high school, when both sides of the family as far back as anyone could remember had been teachers? ("Educators," Bee called them.) But Bee pointed out how lucky he was, knowing so early in life what he wanted and settling in so contentedly. Then Ian readjusted; he shifted gears or something and *whir!* he was rolling along with the others, impressed by Danny's good fortune.

He had always assumed he was the only one who experienced that hitch in his thoughts. He assumed it until the day Lucy arrived, when he felt his parents' hidden start at the word "ex-husband." Wait. The girl of Danny's dreams had chosen someone else before him? And was saddling him with someone else's children besides? His father looked confused. His mother's broad face developed a brittle, tight surface, like something easily broken.

Ian himself absorbed the notion with no trouble. Of course, he wanted only the best for Danny. He had worshiped Danny since infancy—the family's all-round athlete, talented in every known sport but not the least stuck up about it, unfailingly sunny-natured and patient with his little brother. But as Ian saw it, Lucy *was* the best. The ex-husband was only a minor drawback; same for the children. What mattered was that pile of black hair and those long black lashes. None of Danny's previous girls could begin to compare with this one.

But he saw how steadily his parents smiled—stony, glazed smiles as they murmured chitchat. His mother said it certainly was an unusual way for a couple to meet. His father said he'd have opted for parcel post, himself; so *he* would never have been asked to dinner, would he, heh-heh. His mother said that speaking of dinner, Lucy must stay for spaghetti. Danny said she couldn't; he was taking her to Haussner's Restaurant to celebrate their engagement. The word "engagement" sent another shock through the room; for now it was plain that, yes, Danny really was set on this. Bee said maybe later in the week, then. Lucy thanked her in her foggy, fascinating voice. They all stood up. Ian stepped away from the door frame and received his first direct glance from Lucy. She had pure gray eyes, almost silver, and up close her little nose revealed a sprinkling of freckles.

After Danny and Lucy had left, his parents returned to the

living room and sat back down on the couch. Supper was more than ready, but no one mentioned eating. Ian wandered over to the upright piano in the corner. Dozens of family photos, framed in dull brass or varnished wood, stood on an ivory lace runner. Other, larger photos hung behind, nearly obscuring the flowered wallpaper that had darkened over the years to the color of a manila envelope. He studied those: his grandmother standing grimly erect beside his seated grandfather, his Great-Aunt Bess trying to master a hula hoop, Danny in a satin track uniform with a first-place ribbon hung around his neck. Whenever Danny did something he enjoyed, his face would shine with a fine sweat. Even eating made him sweat, or listening to music. And in this photograph—where he'd recently been sprinting under hot sunshine, after all, and then had the pleasure of winning besides—he gleamed; he seemed metallic. You could imagine he was a statue. Ian lightly touched the frame. (Dust felted his finger. For all her great clattery housecleaning, Bee tended to let the little things slide.) Behind him, his mother said, "Well, we've been wishing for years he'd get married."

"That's true, we have," his father said.

"And now that the draft's stepping up . . ."

"Oh, yes, the draft," his father said faintly.

"Did she mention how many children she had?"

"Not that I can recall."

"If she has lots," Bee told him, "we can mix them in with Claudia's and form our own baseball team."

She laughed. Ian turned to look at her, but he was too late. Already she had passed smoothly over to unquestioning delight, and he had missed his chance to see how she did it.

Lucy did not have lots of children after all; just two. A girl aged six and a boy aged three. She lived a couple of miles away, Danny said, in a rented apartment above a Hampden pharmacy; and she left the children with the pharmacist's wife when she went to work every day. He told Ian this later that night, when he stopped by Ian's room on his way to bed. He said she worked as a waitress at the Fill 'Er Up Café—the only job she could find that allowed her to arrange her hours around her children's. But he would soon put an end to *that*, Danny said. No working wife for Danny.

He said she had mailed that package at the request of her ex-husband. Her ex-husband was getting remarried and he wanted her to send him his things. Lucy had packed up every trace of him: the geisha girl figurine he'd won tossing darts at the fair, for instance, and the bowling ball in the red-and-white canvas bag that matched her own. Danny listed these objects in a detailed and lingering way, as if even they had fallen within the circle of his love. The bowling ball, he said, had accounted for much of the package's weight (a total of twenty-eight pounds). Lucy had also mentioned a trophy cup, which couldn't have been so very light either.

Ian tried to imagine Lucy bowling. Illogically, he pictured her in the shoes she had worn to the house—little red pumps with red cloth roses at the toes. The high heels would make tiny dimples in the glossy wood of the runway.

"She's a wonderful cook," Danny said. "Whenever I come to dinner she fixes a special meal for me and she lights new candles. Lucy feels people should always eat by candlelight. And sometimes she makes her own holders; last night it was two red apples. Wasn't that smart? She has the smartest ideas. She's good with napkins, too; she folds them into these different shapes, accordions or butterflies or wigwams, because Lucy says . . ."

Lucy says, Lucy feels, Lucy believes. She seemed almost present in the room with them. Danny lounged in the doorway with his hands in his trouser pockets, his eyes slanting slightly the way they did when something fired him up. The knot of his tie hung loose on his chest, which made him look tipsy even though he wasn't.

How did their evenings *end*? Ian wanted to ask. Did the two of them make out on her couch? Or maybe even go all the way?

Danny spoke of Lucy's knack for interior decorating, her concern for her children, her difficult past life. "Both her parents died in a car crash when she was still in her teens," he said, "and that husband of hers must not have been much, considering how far he's fallen behind on the child support. Not that she complains. She never says a word against anyone; that's not her style. I tell you, Ian, I've been looking for a woman like Lucy all my life, but I'd started to think I'd never find her. I almost thought there was something wrong with me. I'd meet these girls who seemed so pretty and so nice and then it would turn out I'd been hoodwinked; they were flirts or users or constitutional liars and everyone knew it but me. Shouldn't there be some sort of training course in how to judge a woman? How are guys supposed to figure these things out? Well, some just do; it's some kind of gift, I guess. But I was starting to worry I was jinxed. Then along comes Lucy. Two weeks ago she was a total stranger, can you believe it? And yet I'm certain she's the one. She makes her own curtains and she cuts her children's hair herself. She can plant a snipped-off twig in a pot and it will turn green and start growing. When I circle her waist with my hands, my fingertips almost meet."

Ian somehow knew exactly how that would feel: her body narrowing between his palms like a slender, graceful vase.

Danny and Lucy were married a week later, in the Presbyterian church on Dober Street that the Bedloes sporadically attended. Lucy wore a rose-colored suit and a white pillbox hat with a bow. She stood in front of the minister with her arm linked through Danny's, and her feet were placed primly together so that Ian's eyes were riveted to the seams on the backs of her stockings. He had never seen seams on stockings before, if you didn't count old black-and-white movies. He wondered how she got them so straight. They looked like two fountain-pen lines drawn with the aid of a ruler.

Pathetically few guests dotted the bride's side of the church. The first pew held a couple of waitresses from the Fill 'Er Up Café, both wearing cone-shaped hairdos that made them seem the tallest people present. Behind them sat the pharmacist and his wife, with Lucy's two children huddled against the wife. Ian had met the children at a family dinner the night before, and he hadn't thought much of them. Agatha was as cloddish as her name—plain and thick, pasty-faced. Thomas was thin and dark and nimble but no more responsive to grownups. During the wedding they both gazed elsewhere—up at the vaulted ceiling, around at the pebbly pink windows—till Mrs. Myrdal leaned over and whispered sharply. Agatha was the kind of child who breathed through her mouth.

But the groom's side! First came the parents, Doug Bedloe belted in and slicked down in an unfamiliar way and Bee wearing a new striped dress from Hutzler's. Then in the second pew, a row of Daleys—Claudia and her husband, Macy, and all five of their rustling, fidgeting children, even little Ellen, although a sitter had been hired to lurk at the rear of the church just in case. Ian sat in the third pew with Cicely, holding hands. And if he turned around, he could see Danny's friends from high school and his co-workers from the post office and just about the whole neighborhood as well: the Cahns, the Crains, the Mercers, Cicely's parents and her brother Stevie, Mrs. Jordan in her bald fur stole even on this warm May day, and every last one of the foreigners—a row of tan young men wearing identical shiny black suits. The foreigners never missed a chance to attend a celebration.

The minister spoke at some length about the institution of marriage. Danny shifted his weight a few times but Lucy stayed dutifully motionless. Ian wondered why a hat like hers was called a pillbox. It looked more like a pill than a box, he thought—a big white aspirin.

Cicely squeezed his hand and Ian squeezed back, but not as hard. (She was wearing his class ring, bulky as a brass knuckle.) Distantly, he registered the bridal couple's "I do's"—Danny's so emphatic that the younger Daleys giggled, Lucy's throaty and endearing. Then Dr. Prescott pronounced them man and wife, and they kissed. It wasn't one of those show-off kisses you sometimes see at weddings. Lucy just turned and looked up into Danny's eyes, and Danny set both hands on her shoulders and bent to press his lips against hers very gently. After that they stepped back and smiled at the guests, and everyone rose and came forward to offer congratulations.

The reception was held at the Bedloes', with fancy little cakes that Bee and Claudia had been baking for days, and Doug's famous spiked punch in a plastic garbage can reserved only for that purpose, and bottled soft drinks for the children. There were more than enough children. Claudia's brood chased each other through a forest of grownups' legs. Rafe Hamnett's sexy twin ten-year-old daughters stood over by the piano, each slinging out a hip and brandishing a paper straw like a cigarette. Only Lucy's two seemed not to be enjoying themselves. They sat on a windowsill, almost hidden by the curtains on either side. At one point Cicely dragged Ian over to try and make friends with them—she was known at school for being "considerate"—but it wasn't a success. Thomas shrank against his sister and picked at a Band-Aid wrapped around his thumb. Agatha kept her arms folded and stared past them at her mother, who was offering a small hand to each guest as Danny introduced her. ("Honey, this is Melvin Cahn, who lives next door. Melvin, like you to meet the woman who's changed my life.")

Cicely asked Agatha, "Isn't it nice that you have a new uncle? Think of it: Uncle Ian."

Agatha shifted her gaze to Cicely as if it took real effort.

"Isn't that nice?" Cicely said.

Agatha finally nodded.

"She's overcome with joy," Ian told Cicely.

Cicely made a face at him. She was a pert, sweet, round-eyed girl with a bubbly head of blond curls. Today she wore a yellow shift that turned her breasts into two little upturned teacups. Ian laced his fingers through hers and said, "Let's go to your place."

"Go? I haven't said hello to your folks yet."

But she let him lead her away, past Doug Bedloe with his punch dipper poised, past her little brother with his six-gun, past the foreigners practicing their English on the front porch. "Is it not fine day," one of them said—Joe or Jim or Jack; they all had these super-American names shortened from who-knows-what. They stood back respectfully and followed Cicely with their eyes (how they admired blondes!) as Ian guided her down the steps.

Next to the curb, Danny's blue Chevy stood waiting. The bride and groom were driving to Williamsburg for their honeymoon—just a three-day trip because that was the longest Lucy felt comfortable leaving the children. Some of the neighborhood teenagers had tied tin cans to the rear bumper and chalked JUST MARRIED across the trunk. *Married!* Ian thought, and he realized, all at once, that Danny really had gone through with it. He was a husband now and would never again stop by Ian's bedroom door at night, his suit coat hooked over his thumb, to talk about the Baltimore Colts. Ian felt a rush of sorrow. But Cicely's parents wouldn't stay at the reception forever, so he said, "Let's go," and they started walking toward her house.

That summer, Ian got a job with Sid 'n' Ed's A-1 Movers—a very local sort of company consisting of a single van. Each morning he reported to a garage on Greenmount, and then he and two lean, black, jokey men drove to some shabby house where they heaved liquor cartons and furniture into the van for a couple of hours. Then they drove to some other house, often even shabbier, and heaved it all out again. Ian managed to enjoy the work because he thought of it as weight lifting. He had always been very conscious of muscles. As a small boy, admiring Danny and his friends at sports, he had focused upon their forearms—the braiding beneath the skin as they swung a bat or punched a volleyball. There, he thought, was the telling difference, more than whiskers or deep voices. And he had examined his own reedy arms and wondered if they would ever change. But when it happened he must have been asleep, for all at once two summers ago he had noticed as he was mowing the lawn—why, look at that! The ropy muscles from wrist to elbow, the distinct blue cords of his veins. He had flexed a fist and gazed down, hypnotized, till his mother hallooed from the porch and asked how long he planned to stand there.

Well, like a lot of other things, muscles had turned out to be no big deal after all. (Now he thought it might be sleeping with a girl that made the difference.) But even so, he continued to work at building himself up. He deliberately chose the heaviest pieces of furniture, pushing ahead of Lou and LeDon, who were happy to lag behind with the bric-a-brac. Then in the evenings he came home hot and sweaty and swaggery, and his mother would say, "Phew! Go take a shower before you do another thing." He stood under the shower till the water ran cold, after which he dressed in fresh jeans and a T-shirt and went off to eat dinner at Cicely's. His mother hardly cooked at all that summer. Claudia was sick as a dog with her latest pregnancy, so often as not Bee would have spent the day baby-sitting. Sometimes she said, "What, you're eating at the Browns' *again?*" But he could tell she was just as glad. She and his father would have a sandwich in front of the TV, or they'd walk over to Lipton's. She said, "Mind you don't wear out your welcome, now." Then she forgot about him.

He and Cicely twined their feet together under the table while her mother served him double portions of everything. Cicely slid a hand secretly up his thigh, and Ian rearranged his napkin and swallowed and told Mrs. Brown how much he liked her cooking. Mr. Brown was usually absent, out selling insurance to homeowners who could be reached only in the evenings, but Cicely's little brother was there—a pest and a nuisance. He would tag along after dinner, boring Ian to death with baseball questions.

He hung around the two of them on the screened back porch. "*Stee*-vie!" Cicely would say, and Stevie would ask, "What? What am I doing?"

"Don't you have any friends of your own?"

"I'm not doing anything."

"Ma, Stevie's being a brat again."

"Stevie, come along inside, now," Mrs. Brown would call.

Then Stevie would leave, kicking the glider as he passed and lowering his prickly, white-blond head so no one could see his face.

Ian and Cicely had been going together since ninth grade. They were planning to get married after college, although sometimes Cicely teased him and said she'd have to see who else asked her, first. "Change the name and not the letter, change for worse and not for better," she said. But then she would move over into Ian's lap and wrap her arms around his neck. She smelled of baby powder, warm and pink. She wore pink underwear, too— a slippery pink bra with lace edges. Sometimes when they had been kissing a while she would let him unfasten the hook at the back, but he had to be careful not to tickle. She was the most ticklish person he had ever met. Things would just be getting interesting when all at once she would pull away and fall into peals of helpless laughter. Ian felt like a fool when that happened. "Oh, great. Just great," he would say, and she would say, "It's not *my* fault if your hands are cold."

"Cold? It's ninety-eight degrees out."

"That's not *my* fault."

Did other girls behave like this? He would bet they didn't. He wished she were, oh, more womanly, sometimes. More experienced. He said, "This is supposed to be a moment of romantic passion, must I remind you." He said, "We're not in kindergarten, here." Once he said, "Have you ever considered wearing stockings that have seams?" But when Cicely started laughing she just couldn't seem to stop, and all she did was shake her head and wipe the tears from her eyes.

. . .

One August afternoon, he came home from work to find a note on the hall table: *Claudia in hospital, Dad and I staying with kids.* At first he didn't think much about this. Claudia was nearly always in the hospital, it seemed to him, giving birth to one baby or another. He dropped the note in the wastebasket and climbed the stairs, with the dog panting hopefully behind him. But then while he was showering, it occurred to him that Claudia couldn't be having her baby yet. She didn't even look very pregnant yet. He'd better call his mother and find out what was wrong.

As soon as he was dressed, he bounded back downstairs to use the phone. But on the next-to-last step he heard somebody crossing the dining room. Beastie, following close on his heels, uttered a low growl. Then Lucy appeared in the doorway. "Ian?" she said.

"Oh," he said.

She wore a big white shirt of Danny's and a pair of red pedal pushers, and her hair was tied back in a red bandanna. She looked about twelve years old. "Have you talked with your mom yet?" she asked him.

"No, but she left a note. What's the matter with Claudia?"

"Oh, nothing all that serious. Just, you know, a little bleed-ing . . ."

Ian began studying an area slightly above her head.

"So anyway," she said, "I thought I'd fix you some supper. Ordinarily I'd invite you to our place, but we're going out so I brought something over. There's potato salad, and ham, and I've put some peas on the stove to warm up."

He didn't tell her he usually ate at Cicely's. All summer the family had tactfully left her and Danny alone, allowing them to get past the honeymoon stage, so they met only on special oc-casions like Bee's birthday and the Fourth of July. Lucy must not have any notion about their day-to-day lives.

He followed her through the dining room to the kitchen, where he found Thomas and Agatha sitting in two straight-backed chairs. There was something eerie about children who kept so quiet you didn't realize they were in the house. Thomas held a large, naked doll with a matted wig. Agatha's hands were folded tidily on the table in front of her. They looked at Ian with no more expression than the doll wore. Ian said, "Well, hi, gang," but neither of them answered.

He leaned against the sink and watched Lucy flitting around the kitchen. Her hair billowed halfway down her back, longer than he would have expected. She wore white sandals and her toenails were painted fire-engine red. None of the girls at school painted their nails anymore. Everyone was striving for the natural look, which all at once struck Ian as homely.

He realized she must have spoken to him. She was facing him with her head cocked. "Pardon?" he asked.

"Do you want your ham cold, or heated up?"

"Oh, um, cold is fine."

"It won't be real fancy," she said, opening the refrigerator. "Tomorrow if your mom's still busy we'll ask you to dinner. Why, you haven't been over since I painted the living room!"

"No, I guess not," Ian said.

She and Danny were renting a one-story house just north of Cold Spring Lane. So far they had hardly any furniture, but everything they did have was modern, modern, modern—black plastic and aluminum and glass. Bee claimed it would take some getting used to, but Ian loved it.

"Next week I start on the children's room," Lucy said. "I found this magazine with the best ideas! Sit down, why don't you."

He pulled out a chair and sat across from the children. A place had already been laid for him with the company silver and his mother's best china. Two candlesticks from the dining room flanked a bowl of pansies. He began to feel ridiculous, like one of those rich people in cartoons who banquet all alone while a butler stands at the ready. He asked Thomas and Agatha, "Am I the only one eating?"

They gazed at him. Their eyes were a mournful shade of brown.

"How about you?" he asked Thomas's doll. "Won't you join me in a little collation?"

He caught Thomas's lips twitching—a victory. A chink of a giggle escaped him. But Agatha remained unamused. "Her name is Dulcimer," she said reprovingly.

"Dulcimer?"

"Ian doesn't care about all that," Lucy told them.

"She used to have clothes," Agatha said, "but Thomas went and ruined them."

"I did not!" Thomas shouted.

Lucy said, "Ssh," and lit the candles.

"She used to have a dress with two pockets, but he put it in the washer and it came out bits and pieces."

"That was the washer did that, not me!"

"Now she has to go bare, because his other dolls' clothes are too little."

Ian forked up a slice of ham and looked again at Dulcimer. Her body was cloth, soiled to dark gray. Her head was pink vinyl and so were her arms and her legs, which had a wide-set, spraddled appearance. "Maybe she could wear real baby clothes," he suggested.

"Mama won't—"

"That's what I say, too!" Thomas burst out.

"Mama won't let her," Agatha continued stubbornly. There was something unswerving about her. She reminded Ian of certain grade-school teachers he had known. "Mama's got all these baby clothes she buys at Hochschild's, nightgowns and diapers and stuff Dulcimer would *love*, but Mama won't lend them out."

"Have some peas," Lucy told Ian.

"Oh, thanks, I'll just—"

"Today she bought a teeny-weeny baby hat with blue ribbons

but she says if Thomas plays with it he'll get it dirty," Agatha said.

Ian looked over at Lucy, and Lucy looked back at him rue-fully. She said, "Don't tell the others, will you?"

"Okay."

"I want to wait till Claudia gets out of the hospital."

"My lips are sealed," he said.

It was a pleasurable moment, sharing a secret with Lucy. The secret itself, though, he wasn't so sure of. He thought of Danny circling her waist with his hands, his fingertips nearly meeting. Couldn't he have let her stay as she was? Did everything have to keep marching forward all the time?

She said, "We ought to get going, kids."

"Well, thanks for the food," Ian told her.

"You're very welcome."

After they left he could have stopped eating—he was already late for supper at Cicely's—but he worried Lucy would find out somehow and feel hurt. So he made his way through everything, sweating in the candlelight, which was, to tell the truth, sort of uncomfortable for August. She had laid out the ham slices in a careful, scalloped design that reminded him of the patterns etched alongside the ocean. And although it would have saddened him to let the ham go to waste, it saddened him too to finish it and end up with just the empty plate.

Claudia did manage to keep her baby. In fact, she went way past her due date. Her doctor had predicted the first week in Decem-ber, but things dragged on so long that Ian started betting the baby would arrive on his birthday, January 2. "Oh, please," Claudia said. "Let's hope to God you're wrong." She was big as a house and her ankles were swollen and she'd had to have her rings cut off with a hacksaw. At Christmas she was still lumbering around, and Christmas dinner was a spectacle, with Claudia and Lucy sitting elbow to elbow in their ballooning maternity smocks.

Lucy turned out to be the type who carried her baby a great distance in front of her (something to do with her small frame, perhaps), so that even though she had two months to go, she looked nearly as pregnant as Claudia. She was officially a member of the family now—the honeymoon joyfully over and done with, in the Bedloes' eyes, the moment she announced her good news. Now they felt free to stop by her house more often and to invite her and Danny for potluck. Ian had almost reached the point where he could take her for granted. Although still when she turned her silvery gaze upon him he had an arrested feeling, a sense of a skipped beat in the atmosphere of the room.

One of the Bedloe traditions was that important dinners, on holidays and such, were not the usual boring assortment of meats and vegetables. Instead, Bee served their favorite course: hors d'oeuvres. Oh, there'd be a turkey at Thanksgiving, cakes for birthdays, but those were just a nod to convention. What mattered were the stuffed mushrooms, the runny cheeses, the spreads and dips and pâtés and shrimps on toothpicks. The family was secretly proud of this practice; they enjoyed watching guests' reactions. Nothing humdrum about the Bedloes! That Christmas they had oysters on the half shell, and the look of horror on Lucy's children's faces made everybody laugh. "Never mind," Danny told them. "You don't have to eat them if you don't want to."

Danny was exuberant these days. He had researched pregnancy and childbirth as if he expected to deliver the baby himself, and he kept a long scroll of possible names scrunched in his pocket. For some strange reason, he seemed very fond of Thomas and Agatha. Well, Thomas was all right, Ian supposed. He looked kind of cute in his dapper little sailor outfit. But Agatha! Really there was only so much you could do with such a child. Her frilly pink dress made her face appear all the more wooden, and her hair stood out at her jaw in a monolithic wedge. Sometimes Ian caught her giving him one of her flat stares, reminding him of that doll that Thomas was so attached to. Dulcimer. Same numb, blank face, same unseeing eyes.

They moved to the living room and settled themselves, groaning. The cat threw up an oyster behind the couch. Barney fed cracker crumbs to the goldfish, Abbie played "The First Noel" on the piano with a rhythm as ponderous as army boots, and Doug brought out his Polaroid Land camera and took pictures of them all—each photo after the first one showing somebody holding a previous photo, admiring it or grimacing or industriously coating it with fixative. Then little Cindy, who had fallen asleep in front of the fire, woke up cranky, and the dog accidentally stepped on her and made her cry. Claudia said, "That's our cue! Time to go!" and she heaved herself to her feet. They all departed at once—Claudia's family and Danny's—leaving behind a litter of torn gift wrap and mismatched mittens and oyster shells. "This was our best Christmas ever, wasn't it?" Bee asked Doug. But she always said that.

Claudia's baby came two days later—a girl. Frances, they named her. Ian said, "Well, I was *almost* right. It's almost my birthday."

"Cheer up," Bee told him. "There's always the next one."

"Next one! Good grief."

The next one of Claudia's, they both meant. It never occurred to them that *Lucy's* baby might arrive on his birthday. But that was what happened.

He had spent the evening at Cicely's, where she and his friends threw him a party. When he got home he found his mother waiting up for him. "Guess what!" she said. "Lucy had her baby."

"What, so soon?"

"A little girl: Daphne. She's small but healthy, breathing on her own . . . Danny called about an hour ago and he was so excited he could hardly talk."

"After this he won't be fit to live with," Ian said gloomily.

"And Lucy's doing fine. Oh, won't the neighbors tease us? They'll be counting on their fingers, except in this case it's obvious that . . . you want to go with me to the hospital tomorrow?"

"I have school tomorrow," Ian said.

Besides, he had never been much interested in infants.

He didn't see the new baby for a week, in fact, what with one thing and another. Neither did Claudia, who was stuck at home with her own baby. So on Sunday, when everyone gathered at the Bedloes' for dinner, Danny made a big production of introducing his daughter. "Ta-da!" he trumpeted, and he entered the house bearing her high in both hands—a tiny cluster of crochet work. "Here she is, folks! Miss Daphne Bedloe." Lucy looked paler than usual, but she laughed as she bent to unbutton Thomas's jacket.

"Let's see her," Claudia commanded from the couch. She had constructed a kind of nest there and was nursing Franny. Ian had retreated to the other side of the room as soon as he saw Claudia fumbling under her blouse, and he made no move now to come closer. All newborns looked more or less alike, he fig-ured. And this one might still be sort of . . . fetus-shaped. He hung back and dug his hands in his pockets and traced an arc in the rug with one sneaker.

But Danny said, "Don't you want to see too, Ian?" and he sounded so hurt that Ian had to say, "Huh? Oh. Sure." He took his hands from his pockets and approached.

Danny set her on the couch next to Claudia and started peeling off layers. First the crocheted blanket, then an inner blanket, then a bonnet. His fingers seemed too thick for the task, but finally he said, "There!" and straightened up, grinning.

What was that fairy tale? "Sleeping Beauty," maybe, or "Snow White." Skin as white as snow and hair as black as coal and lips as red as roses. So she was prettier than most other babies, yes, but still not all that interesting. Until she opened her eyes.

She opened her eyes and fixed Ian with a thoughtful, con-sidering stare, and Ian felt a sudden loosening in his chest. It seemed she had reached out and pulled a string from somewhere deep inside him. It seemed she *knew* him. He blinked.

"Your birthday-mate," Danny was saying. "Or birthmate, or whatever they call it. Isn't she something?"

To regain his distance, Ian let his eyes slide over to Claudia. He found her looking directly into his face, meaningfully, narrowly. He couldn't think what she wanted to convey; he didn't understand her intensity. Then it came to him, as clearly as if she had spoken.

This is not a premature baby.

He was so astonished that he let his eyes slide back again, forgetting why he had glanced away in the first place. And it was true: she might be small but her cheeks were round, and her little fists were dimpled. She looked nothing like those "Life Before Birth" photos in *Life* magazine.

"Isn't she a love?" Bee asked. "Two loves," she added, blowing a kiss toward Franny. And Claudia said, "She's a beauty, Lucy."

Ian turned to study Claudia. She was smiling now. Her face— a younger, smoother version of Bee's—seemed relaxed and peaceful. The hitch had been smoothed over. Not a trace of it remained. Here was their newest member, born early but in perfect health, thank God, and everything in the Bedloe family was as wonderful as always.

Well, hold on (Ian told himself). Don't be too hasty. Daphne was no longer brand-new, after all. She'd had six whole days to catch up before he laid eyes on her. Best to put the subject right out of his mind.

But over the next few weeks it kept sidling back, somehow.

If Danny and Lucy had been going together forever, why, a seven-months baby (quote, unquote) would have been something to wink at. But they hadn't been going together forever. Nine months ago they hadn't even known each other. Lucy had not yet walked into the post office to plunk her famous package on Danny's counter. She might have been dating someone else entirely.

In school last year a senior had had to get married to a girl he swore he hardly knew. Or rather, he swore *everybody* knew her. It was Ian's first intimation of the fix a man could find himself in. Women were the ones who held the reins, it emerged. Women were up close to things. Men stood off at one remove and were forced to accept women's reading of whatever happened. Probably this was what Ian's father had been trying to tell him in that talk they'd had a few years ago, but Ian hadn't fully understood it at the time.

One night he asked Cicely, "What do you think of Lucy?"

"Oh, I just love her," Cicely said.

"Yes, but—"

"She's always so easy to talk to; she always asks me these questions that show she's been listening. Real questions, I mean. Not those who-cares questions most other grownups ask."

"Yes . . ." Ian said, because he had noticed the same thing himself. Lucy had a grave, focused manner of looking at him. He could imagine she had been reflecting upon him seriously ever since their last meeting.

"I just think Danny is lucky to have her," Cicely said, and Ian said, "Well, yes, he is. Yes, he is lucky."

Ian had quit his job with Sid 'n' Ed's when school reopened; his mother made him. This was his senior year and she wanted him to concentrate on getting into a halfway decent college. The last thing he needed was to waste his time hauling other people's mattresses, she said.

But what she didn't seem to realize was that a person his age had to have a social life, and a social life took money. By February, he was broke. So when Lucy called and asked if he would baby-sit—a job he hated, and one he was ill equipped for besides, as youngest in his family—he didn't immediately refuse. "Well," he said, stalling, "but I don't even know how to change a diaper."

"You wouldn't have to," Lucy told him. "I would change her just before I left. And most likely she'd be sleeping; this would be afternoons."

"Oh. Afternoons."

"Just a couple of hours after school now and then. Please, Ian? I'm about to lose my mind cooped up all day. And I can't keep imposing on your mother, and Mrs. Myrdal won't come anymore and Cicely's got cheerleading practice. I just want to get out on my own a while—go shopping or take a walk with nobody hanging onto me. I'd pay you a dollar an hour."

"You would?" he said.

On the rare occasions Claudia had talked him into sitting, the pay had been fifty cents.

"And Thomas and Agatha have taken such a shine to you. They're the ones who suggested you."

"Oh, well, in that case," Ian said. "If it's a matter of popular demand . . ."

So he started walking over from school one or two afternoons a week and staying till dusk. It wasn't a job that required much work, but somehow he found it far more tiring than Sid 'n' Ed's. No wonder Lucy wanted a break! This was the coldest, grayest time of year, and the stark modern furniture that had seemed so elegant in the summer had a bleak feel in the winter. Toys and picture books covered the white vinyl couch. Sheaves of Agatha's pulpy first-grade papers lay scattered across the rug. Thomas and Agatha had the used, slightly tarnished look that even the best-tended children take on late in the day, and they pressed in upon him too closely, drilling him with questions. Was Ian ever going to play in the World Series? Did he know how to drive a car? A motorcycle? An airplane? Did he and Cicely go to many balls? (This last from Agatha, who had a big crush on Cicely.) Gradually he forgot that they had once been tongue-tied in his presence.

They clung to the belief that Ian felt a special affection for Dulcimer, and they always made a point of displaying what she was wearing that day—one or another infant outfit handed down from Daphne. "Why, Miss Dulcimer!" Ian would say. "I do believe fuzzy pink flannel is your most becoming fabric." They thought it was hilarious when he spoke to her directly. Then they might play Parcheesi—Ian's idea; all the Bedloes loved any kind of game—or he read to them, his throat aching tightly with held-back yawns as he imitated various squeaky animals.

Daphne was usually an invisible, slumbering presence, but if Lucy stayed out too long Ian might hear a tentative cry from the children's room. He would find her lying in her crib, sucking her fist and watching the door so his first impression was always that considering stare. She was the only person he knew of with navy blue eyes. He would lift her awkwardly, in a bunch, pretending not to notice the dampness seeping around the legs of her terry-cloth pajamas. He would carry her to the kitchen and set a bottle in the electric warmer. Waiting for it to heat, he breathed her smell of warm urine and something vanilla-ish— maybe just her skin. Thomas tugged at one of her terry-cloth feet. "Hey there, Daffy. Daffy-doo." Daphne squirmed and murmured into the curve of Ian's neck.

When Lucy returned, she brought a burst of cold air through the door with her. The cold seemed to lie on her surface in a sparkling film. And she was always lit up and laughing, excited by her expedition. She would hold out her arms to the children. "Were you good?" she would ask. "Did you miss me?" and she'd take the baby from Ian and nuzzle her face, nose to nose. "Guess what: I felt a couple of snowflakes. I bet we're going to have snow tonight." Balancing Daphne on her hip, she would fish in her big shoulder bag for Ian's pay—generously rounding off to the nearest dollar, sometimes even adding a tip and telling him to take Cicely someplace nice. Ian knew that she and Danny weren't rich, and he would protest but she always insisted. "Well, thanks," he'd say lamely, and she would say, "Thank *you!* You don't know how you saved my life." Her money smelled of her cologne, a tingly scent that clung to the bills for hours afterward and hung in his room when he emptied his pockets at bedtime.

One afternoon when she returned there was something distracted about her. She greeted the children absently and failed to inquire beside her and run through a lot of everyday, wife-ish remarks. She said, 'Don't forget the garbage,' and, 'Suppertime!' and, 'You're late.' Her theory was, the name would sort of swim into Agatha's memory. She thought Thomas was too young to try it on. But all at once Thomas pipes up, 'You're late with the check again, Tom!' he said. Just out of nowhere!"

"Well, that would make sense," Ian said. "So Thomas must be Tom Junior."

"I said to Jessie Jordan, I said, 'Jessie,' I said, 'you're amazing.' Really I don't know what I'd have done without her, these past few days. Or *any* of the neighbors. They've all been so helpful, running errands for me and taking the children when my legs are bad . . ."

What she was saying, it seemed to Ian, was, "See what you've gone and done? See how you've ruined our lives?" Although of course she didn't mean that at all. She went on to say the Cahns, next door, had lent her their sitter, and the foreigners had brought over a pot of noodle soup with an aftertaste resembling throw-up. "People have been just lovely," she said, "and Cicely's mother called to say—"

"But what about Thomas Senior?" Ian broke in.

"What about him?"

"Did you look for him in the Cheyenne phone book?"

"Oh, we'd already called all the Deans in Cheyenne, but now we have a name to give the officials. They ought to be able to track *something* down—driver's license, marriage license . . . I remember Lucy said once he'd remarried."

That night Ian dreamed that Lucy sat in her living room among bushel baskets of mail—letters and fliers and magazines. Then Danny walked in and said, "Lucy? What is this?"

"Oh," she said, "I just can't open them anymore. Since you died it seems I haven't had the heart."

"But this is terrible!" he cried. "Your bulks and your flats I could understand, but first-class, Lucy! First-class envelopes lying untouched!"

"Then talk to Ian," she said in a wiry, tight voice.

"Ian?"

"Ian says I'm not a bit first-class," she said, and her mouth turned down at the corners, petulant and spiteful looking.

Ian awoke and blinked at the crack of light beneath the door. Winston was snoring. Someone's radio was playing. He heard the scrape of a chair down the hall and carefree, unthinking laughter.

Sunday morning he rode into town on the college's little blue church bus. Most of the passengers were students he'd never laid eyes on before, although he did recognize his lab partner, dressed in a hard-surfaced, voluminous gray coat. He pretended not to see her and proceeded toward the long seat at the rear, where he settled between two boys with haircuts so short and suits so tidy that they might have stepped out of the 1950s. Really this was a sort of *losers'* bus, he realized, and he had an impulse to jump off while he still could. But then the senior class secretary boarded—a poised, attractive girl—and he felt reassured. He rode through the stubbled farmlands with his eyes fixed straight ahead, while the boy on his left fingered a rosary and the boy on his right whispered over a Bible.

At the courthouse square in Sumner, the bus stopped and everyone disembarked. Ian chose to follow the largest group of students, which included the senior class secretary and also a relatively normal-looking freshman named Eddie something whom he'd seen around the dorm. He and Eddie fell into step together, and Eddie said, "You on your way to Leeds Memorial?"

"Well, yeah, I guess so."

Eddie nodded. "It's not too bad," he said. "I go every week on account of my grandmother's paying me."

"Paying you?"

"If I don't miss a Sunday all year I get a check for a hundred bucks."

"Gosh," Ian said.

Leeds Memorial was a stately brick building with a white interior and dark, varnished pews. The choir sounded professional, and they sang the opening hymn on their own while the congregation stayed seated. Maybe that was why Ian didn't have much feeling about it. It was only music, that was all—something unfamiliar, classical-sounding, flawlessly performed. Maybe the whole church had to be singing along.

The theme of the day was harvest, because they were drawing close to Thanksgiving. The Bible reading referred to the reaping of grain, and the sermon had to do with resting after one's labors. The pastor—a slouching, easygoing, just-one-of-the-guys type with a sweater vest showing beneath his suit coat—counseled his listeners to be kind to themselves, to take time for themselves in the midst of the hurly-burly. Ian felt enormous yawns hollowing the back of his throat. Finally the organist began thrumming out a series of chords, and the sermon came to an end and everyone rose. The hymn was "Bringing in the Sheaves." It was a simpleminded, seesawing sort of tune, Ian felt, and the collective voice of the congregation had a note of fluty gentility, as if dominated by the dressed-up old ladies lining the pews.

Walking back to the bus, Eddie asked if he'd be coming every Sunday.

Ian said he doubted it.

His Thanksgiving vacation was fractious and disorganized; Lucy's children had still not been claimed. By now they had moved in upon the household in full force. Their toys littered the living room, their boats and ducks crowded the bathroom, and Daphne's real crib—much larger than the Port-a-Crib—cramped his bedroom. He was alarmed at how haggard his mother looked, and how heavy and big-bellied. The waistband of her slacks was extended with one of those oversized safety pins women once decorated their kilts with. And the holiday dinner she served was halfhearted—no hors d'oeuvres, not even beforehand, and the turkey unstuffed and the pies store-bought. Even the company seemed lacking. Claudia snapped at her children, Macy kept drifting away from the table to watch a football game on TV, and the foreigners had to leave before dessert in order to meet the plane of a new arrival. All in all, it was a relief to have the meal over with.

He tried to help with the children as much as possible. He played endless games of Parcheesi; he read and reread *The Sad Little Bunny*. And he rose at least once each night to rock Daphne back to sleep, sometimes nodding off himself in the process. Often he had the feeling that she was rocking *him*. He would wake to find her coolly studying his face in the dark, or even prying up one of his lids with her chubby, sticky fingers.

Ironically, it was during this vacation that Cicely told him she might be pregnant. In the middle of a movie called *Georgy Girl*, which concerned a young woman who was tiresomely, tediously fond of infants, she clutched a handful of his sleeve and whispered that she was two weeks late. "Late for what?" he asked, which for some reason made her start crying. Then he understood.

They walked out on the movie and drove around the city. Ian kept inventing other possibilities. She was tense about her exams, maybe, or it was all that traveling back and forth on the train, or—"I don't know! How would I know? *Some* damn reason!" he said, and she said, "You don't have to shout! It was your fault as much as it was mine! Or more, even; way more. You're the one who talked me into it."

This wasn't entirely accurate. Still, on some deeper level it seemed he deserved every word she hurled at him. He saw himself as a plotter and a predator, sex-obsessed; Lord, there were days when thoughts of sex with anyone—it didn't have to be Cicely— never left his mind for a moment. And now look: here was his rightful penance, marriage at eighteen and a job bagging groceries in the A&P. He drew a breath. He said, "Don't worry, Ciss. I'll take care of you."

They were supposed to stop by Andrew's after the movie, but instead he drove her home. "I'll call you tomorrow," he said, and then he went on to his own house and climbed the stairs to his room, where he found Daphne sitting upright and holding out her arms.

By the time he returned to school on Sunday evening, he had almost persuaded Cicely to see a doctor. What he hoped for (although he didn't say it) was a doctor who could offer her a magic pill or something. There must be such a pill. Surely there was. Maybe it was some common cold remedy or headache tablet, available on open shelves, with NOT TO BE TAKEN DURING PREGNANCY imprinted on the label—a message in code for those who needed it. But if he mentioned this to Cicely she might think he didn't want to marry her or something, when of course he did want to and had always planned to. Just not yet, please, God. Not when he'd never even slept with a *dark*-haired girl yet.

He flinched at the wickedness of this thought, which had glided so smoothly into his mind that it might have been there all along.

In Biology 101 on Tuesday, his lab partner said she'd noticed him on the church bus. She wondered if he'd like to attend the Wednesday Night Youth Group at her place of worship. "Oh, I'm sorry, I can't," he said instantly. "I've got a paper due."

"Well, maybe another time, then," she said. "We always have such fun! Usually they show a movie, something nice and clean with no language."

"It does sound like fun," he said.

He meant that sincerely. He ached, all at once, for a blameless life. He decided that if Cicely turned out not to be pregnant, *they* would start living like that. Their outings would become as wholesome as those pictures in the cigarette ads: healthy young people laughing toothily in large, impersonal groups, popping popcorn, taking sleigh rides.

But on Thursday, when Cicely phoned to tell him she'd got her period, what did he do? He said, "Listen. You have to go on the pill now. You know that." And she said, "Yes, I've already made an appointment." And that weekend they picked up where they had left off, although Cicely still had her period and really it was sort of complicated. He had to rinse all the bedclothes the following morning, and as he stood barefoot in the dormitory bathroom watching the basin fill with pink water, he felt weary and jaded and disgusted with himself, a hopeless sinner.

Christmas fell on a Sunday that year. Ian didn't get home till Friday evening; so Saturday was a hectic rush of shopping for gifts. Only on Christmas Eve did he have a chance to look around and realize the state of the household. He saw that although a good-sized tree had been erected in the living room, no one had trimmed it; the box of decorations sat unopened on the piano. The swags of evergreen were missing from the banister, the front door bore no wreath, and the house had a general air of neglect. It wasn't just relaxed, or folksy, or happy-go-lucky; it was dirty. The kitchen smelled of garbage and cat box. The last two remaining goldfish floated dead in their scummy bowl. None of the gifts had been wrapped yet, and when the children asked to hang their stockings it emerged that all the socks were in the laundry.

"Well, I'm sorry," Bee said, "but one person or another has been sick the last two weeks running and I just haven't had a minute. So I'm sorry. Hang something else, instead. Hang grocery bags. Hang pillowcases."

"Pillowcases!" Thomas said dolefully.

"Don't worry," Ian told him. "I'll do a wash tonight. You go on to bed and I'll hang your stockings later."

So that evening was spent in the basement, more or less. Ian found the hampers so overstuffed and moldy that he guessed the laundry had not been seen to in some time, and he decided to take care of the whole lot. Also he put himself in charge of gift wrapping. While his mother sat at the dining room table sipping the sherry he'd poured her, he swaddled everything ineptly in plain tissue. (She had not thought to buy Christmas paper.) He wrapped even the gifts meant for him—a couple of shirts, a ski jacket—pretending to pay them no heed. Periodically he left his work to run downstairs to the basement and start another load of laundry. The scent of detergent and fresh linens gradually filled the house. It wasn't such a bad Christmas Eve after all.

"Remember Christmas in the old days?" his mother asked. "When we got everything ready so far ahead? Presents sat under the tree for weeks! Homemade, most of them. Lord, you children made enough clay ashtrays to cover every surface, and none of us even smokes. But this year I just couldn't get up the spirit. Seems like ever since this happened with your brother I've been so . . . unenthusiastic."

Ian didn't know what to say to that. He made a big business of tying a bow on a package.

"And remember all the hors d'oeuvres at Christmas dinner?" she asked. "This year I'll be doing well to throw a piece of meat in the oven."

"Maybe we should go to a restaurant," Ian said.

"A restaurant!"

"Why not?"

"Let's hope we haven't come to *that*," his mother said.

In the living room they heard a sharp grunt—his father, asleep in his recliner chair.

But as it turned out, Christmas Day was not so different that year from any other. Mrs. Jordan came, along with the foreigners. The children contributed their share of excitement (Claudia's six and Lucy's three, combined), and Doug's Polaroid Land camera flashed, and the cat made choking sounds behind the couch. It was disconcerting, in a way. Last Christmas Daphne hadn't been born yet; nor had Franny. Now here sat Daphne chewing a wad of blue tissue while Franny stirred her fists through Agatha's jigsaw puzzle. They both seemed so accustomed to being here. And Danny and Lucy had completely vanished. Something was wrong with a world where people came and went so easily.

The day after Christmas, Sid at the movers' phoned to see if

Ian could help out over vacation. Their man Brewster had left them in the lurch, he said. Ian told him he'd be glad to help. School would not reopen till mid-January and he could use the extra cash. So Tuesday morning, he reported to the garage on Greenmount.

LeDon was delighted to see him. That Brewster fellow, he said, had just up and walked away in the middle of a job. "He say, 'See you round, LeDon.' I say, 'Hey, man, you ain't *ditching* me.' He say, 'All day long I'm ditching you,' and off he go. Well, he won't never what you call real friendly."

They were moving an old lady from a house to an apartment—lots of old-lady belongings, bowlegged furniture and mothballed dresses and more than enough china to stock a good-sized restaurant. Her son, who was overseeing the move, had some kind of fixation about the china. "Careful, now! That's Spode," he would say as they lifted a crate. And, "Watch out for the Haviland!" LeDon rolled his eyes at Ian.

Then at the new place, they found out the kitchen was being remodeled and they had to set the china crates in the living room. "What the hell?" the son said. "This was supposed to be finished three days ago." He was talking to the cabinetmaker—the deaf man Ian had come across last summer, as it happened. "How much longer?" the son asked him. Any fool could see it would be *way* longer; the kitchen was nothing but a shell. The cabinetmaker, not looking around, measured the depth of a counter with a steel measuring tape. The son laid a hand on the man's forearm. The man turned slowly, gazed a moment at the son's hand, and then lifted his eyes to his face. "HOW . . . LONG!" the son shouted, exaggerating his lip movements.

The cabinetmaker considered, and then he said, "Two weeks."

"Two weeks!" the son said. He dropped his hand. "What are you building here, Noah's ark? All we need is a few lousy cupboards!"

The cabinetmaker went on about his business, measuring the

counter's length now and the height of the empty space above it. Surely he must have known the son was speaking to him, but he seemed totally absorbed in what he was doing. Once again, Ian envied the man his insular, impervious life.

On New Year's Eve Pig Benson threw a big, rowdy party, but Ian didn't go. Cicely was baby-sitting her brother and it was her last night home. (Her college worked on a different schedule from Ian's.) So they set all the clocks an hour ahead and tricked Stevie into going to bed early, and then they snuck upstairs to her room, where Ian unintentionally dozed off. He was awakened by church bells ringing in the New Year, which meant her parents could be expected at any moment. As soon as he'd dressed, he slipped downstairs and into the frosty, bitter night. He walked home half asleep while bells pealed and firecrackers popped and rockets lit the sky. What optimism! he found himself thinking. Why did people have such high hopes for every New Year?

He practiced saying the date aloud: "Nineteen sixty-seven. January first, nineteen sixty-seven." Monday was his birthday; he'd be nineteen years old. Daphne would be one. He shivered and pulled his collar up.

That night he dreamed Danny came driving down Waverly Street in Sumner College's blue church bus. He stopped in front of home and told Ian, "They've given me a new route and now I get to go anywhere I like."

"Can I ride along?" Ian asked from the sidewalk.

"You can ride along after you learn Chinese," Danny told him.

"Oh," Ian said. Then he said, "Chinese?"

"Well, I like to call it Chinese."

"Call what Chinese?"

"You understand, Chinese is not what I really mean."

"Then what *do* you mean?" Ian asked.

"Why, I'm talking about . . . let us say . . . Chinese," Danny said, and he winked at Ian and laughed and drove away.

When Ian woke, Daphne was crying, and the room seemed moist as a greenhouse from her tears.

Agatha's school reopened Tuesday, and Thomas's nursery school Wednesday. This should have lightened Bee's load, but still she looked exhausted every evening. She said she must have a touch of the flu. "Ordinarily I'm strong as a horse!" she said. "This is only temporary, I'm positive."

Ian asked, "What's the word on Tom Dean, Senior? Any sign of him?"

"Oh," his mother said, "I guess we'll have to give up on Tom Dean. It doesn't seem he exists."

"Then what'll you do with the children?"

"Well, your father has some ideas. He's pretty sure from something Lucy once mentioned that she came from Pennsylvania. Maybe her first marriage was recorded there, he says, in which case—"

"You're stuck with them, aren't you," Ian said.

"Pardon?"

"You're stuck with those children for good."

"Oh, no," she told him. "I'm certain we'll find somebody sooner or later. We'll just have to. We'll have to!"

"But what if you don't?" Ian asked her.

Her face took on a flown-apart, panicked look.

Two of the children weren't even Bedloes, and he wondered if it occurred to his parents that those two could simply be made wards of the state, or whatever—popped into some kind of foster home or orphanage. But he suspected that with Daphne, they wouldn't feel free to do that. Daphne was their dead son's child, and an infant besides. She wasn't already formed, as the other two were. She hadn't yet reached the knobby-kneed, scabby stage that only a mother could love; she was still full of dimples, still tiny and beguiling.

Thomas, on the other hand, could cause a serious puncture wound if he accidentally poked you with his elbow. Holding him on your lap was like holding a bunch of coat hangers. Which didn't prevent his trying to climb up there, heaven knows. He had the nuzzling, desperate manner of a small dog starved for attention, which unfortunately lessened his appeal; while Agatha, who managed to act both sullen and ingratiating, came across as sly. Ian had seen how grownups (even his mother, even his earth-mother sister) turned narrow-eyed in Agatha's presence. It seemed that only Ian knew how these children felt: how scary they found every waking minute.

Why, being a child at all was scary! Wasn't that what grown-ups' nightmares so often reflected—the nightmare of running but getting nowhere, the nightmare of the test you hadn't studied for or the play you hadn't rehearsed? Powerlessness, outsiderness. Murmurs over your head about something everyone knows but you.

He finished moving a family into a row house on York Road and went home from there on foot, passing a series of shabby stores. The job had run unusually late. It was after seven on a dismal January evening, and most places had closed. One window, though, glowed yellow—a wide expanse of plate glass with CHURCH OF THE SECOND CHANCE arching across it in block letters. Ian couldn't see inside because the paper shade was lowered. He walked on by. Behind him a hymn began. "Something something something lead us . . ." He missed most of the words, but the voices were strong and joyful, overlaid by a single tenor that rose above the rest.

He paused at the intersection, the arches of his sneakers teetering on the curb. He peered at the DON'T WALK sign for a moment. Then he turned and headed back to the church.

A shopkeeper's bell jingled when he opened the door. The singers looked around—some fifteen or twenty people, standing in rows with their backs to him—and smiled before they looked

away again. They were facing a tall, black-haired man in a tieless
white shirt and black trousers. The pulpit was an ordinary store
counter. The floor was green linoleum. The lights overhead were
long fluorescent tubes and one tube flickered rapidly, giving Ian
the impression that he had a twitch in his eyelid.

"Blessed Jesus! Blessed Jesus!" the congregation sang. It was
a tender, affectionate cry that sounded personally welcoming.
Ian found his way to an empty spot beside a woman in a white
uniform, a nurse or a waitress. Although she didn't look at him,
she moved closer and angled her hymnal so he could follow the
words. The hymnal was one of those pocket-sized pamphlets
handed out free at public sing-alongs. There wasn't any accom-
paniment, not even a piano. And the pews—as Ian realized when
the hymn came to an end and everyone sat down—were plain
gray metal folding chairs, the kind you'd see at a bridge game.

"Friends," the minister said, in a sensible, almost conversational tone. "And guests," he added, nodding at Ian. All over
again, the others turned and smiled. Ian smiled back, maybe a
little too broadly. He had the feeling he was their first and only
visitor.

"We have reached that point in the service," the minister
said, "when any person here is invited to step forward and ask
for our prayers. No request is too great, no request is trivial in
the eyes of God our Father."

Ian thought of the plasterer who'd repaired his parents' bathroom ceiling. NO JOB TOO LARGE OR TOO SMALL, his panel truck
had read. He brushed the thought away. He watched a very fat
young woman heave herself to her feet just in front of him. The
width of her sprigged, summer-weight skirt, when she finally
reached a standing position, completely blocked his view of the
minister. "Well, Clarice as you may have heard is down real bad
with her blood," she said breathily. "We had thought that was
all behind her but now it's come on back, and I asked what I
could do for her and she says, 'Lynn,' says, 'take it to Wednesday
Night Prayer Meeting, Lynn, and ask them for their prayers.' So
that's just what I'm doing."

There was a silence, during which she sat down. As soon as she left Ian's line of vision, he realized the silence was part of the program. The minister stood with both palms raised, his face tipped skyward and his eyelids closed and gleaming. In his shirt-sleeves, he seemed amateurish. His cuffs had slipped down his forearms, and his collar, Ian saw, was buttoned all the way to the neck, in the fashion of those misfits who used to walk around high school with slide rules dangling from their belts. He wasn't so very old, either. His frame was lanky as a marionette's and his wrist bones boyishly knobby.

Ian was the only one sitting erect. He bowed his head and squinted at the billow of sprigged skirt puffing out the back of the fat woman's chair.

"For our sister Clarice," the minister said finally.

"Amen," the congregation murmured, and they straightened.

"Any other prayers, any other prayers," the minister said. "No request is beyond Him."

On the other side of Ian's neighbor, a gray-haired woman rose and placed her purse on her seat. Then she faced forward, gripping the chair in front of her. "You all know my son Chuckie was fighting in Vietnam," she said.

There were nods, and several people turned to look at her.

"Well, now they tell me he's been killed," she said.

Soft sounds of dismay traveled down the rows.

"Tell me he got killed jumping out of a plane," she said. "You know he was a paratrooper."

More nods.

"Monday night these two soldiers came, all dressed up."

"Ah, no," they said.

"I told them I had thought he'd be safe. I said he'd been jumping so *long* now, looked to me like he'd learned how to stay alive up there. Soldier says, 'Yes, ma'am,' he says. 'These things happen,' he says. Says Chuckie was a, what do you call, fluke accident. Forgot to put his parachute on."

Ian blinked.

"Forgot!" his neighbor marveled in a voice like a dove.

" 'Forgot!' I said. 'How could that be?' This soldier tells me, it's the army's considered opinion that Chuckie had just jumped so often, he'd stopped thinking about it. So up he comes to that whatever, that door where they jump out of, the whole time making smart remarks so everybody's laughing—you remember what a card he was—and gives a little kind of like salute and steps into empty air. It's not till then the fellow behind him says, 'Wait!' Says, 'Wait, you forgot your—' "

"Parachute," Ian's neighbor finished sadly.

"So I don't ask your prayers for Chuckie after this; I ask for me," the woman said. For the first time, her voice was unsteady. "I'm just about sick with grief, I tell you. Pray for me to find some deliverance."

She sat down, fumbling behind her for her purse. The minister lifted his palms and the room fell silent.

Could you really forget your parachute?

Well, maybe so. Ian could see how it might have come about. A man to whom jumping was habit might imagine that floating in space was all his own doing, like flying. Maybe it had slipped his mind he *couldn't* fly, so in the first startled instant of his descent he supposed he had simply forgotten how. He may have felt insulted, betrayed by all he'd taken for granted. *What's the big idea here?* he must have asked.

Ian pictured one of those animated films where a character strolls off a cliff without noticing and continues strolling in mid-air, perfectly safe until he happens to look down and then his legs start wheeling madly and he plummets.

He gave a short bark of laughter.

The congregation swiveled and stared at him.

He bowed his head, cheeks burning. The minister said, "For our sister Lula."

"Amen," the others said, mercifully facing forward again.

"Any other prayers, any other prayers . . ."

Ian studied the sprigged skirt while shame slammed into him in waves. He had said and done heedless things before but this was something new: to laugh out loud at a mother's bereavement.

He wished he could disappear. He wanted to perform some violent and decisive act, like leaping into space himself.

"No prayer is unworthy in the eyes of our Creator."

He stood up.

Heads swiveled once again.

"I used to be—" he said.

Frog in his throat. He gave a dry, fake-sounding cough.

"I used to be good," he said. "Or I used to be not bad, at least. Not evil. I just *assumed* I wasn't evil, but lately, I don't know what's happened. Everything I touch goes wrong. I didn't mean to laugh just now. I'm sorry I laughed, Mrs. . . ."

He looked over at the woman. Her face was lowered and she seemed unaware of him. But the others were watching closely. He had the sense they were weighing his words; they were taking him seriously.

"Pray for me to be good again," he told them. "Pray for me to be forgiven."

He sat down.

The minister raised his palms.

The silence that followed was so deep that Ian felt bathed in it. He unfolded in it; he gave in to it. He floated on a fluid rush of prayers, and all the prayers were for his pardon. How could God not listen, then?

When Ian was three or four years old, his mother had read him a Bible story for children. The illustration had showed a Roman soldier in full armor accosting a bearded old man. "Is that God?" Ian had asked, pointing to the soldier; for he associated God with power. But his mother had said, "No, no," and continued reading. What Ian had gathered from this was that God was the other figure, therefore—the bearded old man. Even after he knew better, he couldn't shake that notion, and now he imagined the congregation's prayers streaming toward someone with long gray hair and a floor-length, Swedish-blue robe and sturdy bare feet in leather sandals. He felt a flood of gratitude to this man, as if God were, in literal truth, his father.

"For our guest," the minister said.

"Amen."

It was over too suddenly. It hadn't lasted long enough. Already the minister was saying, "Any other prayers, any other prayers . . ."

There weren't any.

"Hymn sixteen, then," the minister said, and everyone stirred and rustled pages and stood up. They were so matter-of-fact; they were smoothing skirts, patting hairdos. Ian's neighbor, a stocky, round-faced woman, beamed at him and tilted her hymnal in his direction. The hymn was "Leaning on the Everlasting Arms." The minister started it off in his soaring tenor:

> "What a fellowship, what a joy divine,
> Leaning on the everlasting arms . . ."

This time Ian sang too, although really it was more of a drone.

When the hymn was finished, the minister raised his palms again and recited a benediction. "Go ye now into the world and bear witness to His teachings," he said. "In Jesus' name, amen."

"Amen," the others echoed.

Was that *it*?

They started collecting coats and purses, buttoning buttons, winding scarves. "Welcome!" Ian's neighbor told him. "How did you find out about us?"

"Oh, I was just walking by . . ."

"So many young people nowadays don't give half enough thought to their spiritual salvation."

"No, I guess not," Ian said.

All at once he felt he was traveling under false pretense. Spiritual salvation! The language these places used made him itch with embarrassment. (Blood of the Lamb, Died for Your Sins . . .) He looked yearningly behind him, where the first people to leave were already sending a slap of cold air into the room. But his neighbor was waving to the minister. "Yoo-hoo! Reverend Emmett! Come and meet our young person!"

The minister, already choosing a path between the knots of worshipers, seemed disconcertingly jubilant. His smile was so wide that his teeth looked too big for his mouth. He arrived in front of Ian and shook his hand over and over. "Wonderful to have you!" he said. (His long, bony fingers felt like dried bean-pods.) "I'm Reverend Emmett. This is Sister Nell, have you introduced yourselves?"

"How do you do," Ian said, and the other two waited so expectantly that he had to add, "I'm Ian Bedloe."

"We use only first names in our place of worship," Reverend Emmett told him. "Last names remind us of the superficial— the world of wealth and connections and who came over on the *Mayflower*."

"Really," Ian said. "Ah. Okay."

His neighbor laid a hand on his arm and said, "Reverend Emmett will tell you *all about it*. Nice meeting you, Brother Ian. Good night, Reverend Emmett."

"Night," Reverend Emmett said. He watched as she swirled a navy cape around her shoulders (so she was, after all, a nurse) and sidled out the other end of the row. Then he turned back to Ian and said, "I hope your prayer was answered this evening."

"Thanks," Ian said. "It was a really . . . interesting service."

Reverend Emmett studied him. (His skin was an unhealthy shade of white, although that could have been the fluorescent lighting.) "But your prayer," he said finally. "Was there any response?"

"Response."

"Did you get a reply?"

"Well, not exactly."

"I see," Reverend Emmett said. He watched an aged couple assist each other through the door—the very last to leave. Then he said, "What was it that you needed forgiven?"

Ian couldn't believe his ears. Was this even legal, inquiring into a person's private prayers? He ought to spin on his heel and walk out. But instead his heart began hammering as if he were about to do something brave. In a voice not quite his own, he said, "I caused my brother to, um, kill himself."

Reverend Emmett gazed at him thoughtfully.

"I told him his wife was cheating on him," Ian said in a rush, "and now I'm not even sure she was. I mean I'm pretty sure she did in the past, I know I wasn't *totally* wrong, but . . . So he drove into a wall. And then his wife died of sleeping pills and I guess you could say I caused that too, more or less . . ."

He paused, because Reverend Emmett might want to disagree here. (Really Lucy's death was just indirectly caused by Ian, and maybe not even that. It might have been accidental.) But Reverend Emmett only rocked from heel to toe.

"So it looks as if my parents are going to have to raise the children," Ian said. Had he mentioned there were children? "Everything's been dumped on my mom and I don't think she's up to it—her or my dad, either one. I don't think they'll ever be the same, after this. And my sister's busy with her own kids and I'm away at college most of the time . . ."

In the light of Reverend Emmett's blue eyes—which had the clean transparency of those marbles that Ian used to call gingerales—he began to relax. "So anyhow," he said, "that's why I asked for that prayer. And I honestly believe it might have worked. Oh, it's not like I got an answer in plain English, of course, but . . . don't you think? Don't you think I'm forgiven?"

"Goodness, no," Reverend Emmett said briskly.

Ian's mouth fell open. He wondered if he'd misunderstood. He said, "I'm *not* forgiven?"

"Oh, no."

"But . . . I thought that was kind of the point," Ian said. "I thought God forgives everything."

"He does," Reverend Emmett said. "But you can't just say, 'I'm sorry, God.' Why, anyone could do that much! You have to offer reparation—concrete, practical reparation, according to the rules of our church."

"But what if there isn't any reparation? What if it's something nothing will fix?"

"Well, that's where Jesus comes in, of course."

Another itchy word: Jesus. Ian averted his eyes.

"Jesus remembers how difficult life on earth can be," Reverend Emmett told him. "He helps with what you can't undo. But only after you've *tried* to undo it."

"Tried? Tried how?" Ian asked. "What would it take?"

Reverend Emmett started collecting hymnals from the chair seats. Apparently he was so certain of the answer, he didn't even have to think about it. "Well, first you'll need to see to those children," he said.

"Okay. But . . . see to them in what way, exactly?"

"Why, raise them, I suppose."

"Huh?" Ian said. "But I'm only a freshman!"

Reverend Emmett turned to face him, hugging the stack of hymnals against his concave shirt front.

"I'm away in Pennsylvania most of the time!" Ian told him.

"Then maybe you should drop out."

"Drop out?"

"Right."

"Drop out of college?"

"Right."

Ian stared at him.

"This is some kind of test, isn't it?" he said finally.

Reverend Emmett nodded, smiling. Ian sagged with relief.

"It's God's test," Reverend Emmett told him.

"So . . ."

"God wants to know how far you'll go to undo the harm you've done."

"But He wouldn't really make me follow through with it," Ian said.

"How else would He know, then?"

"Wait," Ian said. "You're saying God would want me to give up my education. Change all my parents' plans for me and give up my education."

"Yes, if that's what's required," Reverend Emmett said.

"But that's crazy! I'd have to be crazy!"

" 'Let us not love in word, neither in tongue,' " Reverend Emmett said, " 'but in deed and in truth.' First John three, eighteen."

"I can't take on a bunch of kids! Who do you think I am? I'm nineteen years old!" Ian said. "What kind of a cockeyed religion *is* this?"

"It's the religion of atonement and complete forgiveness," Reverend Emmett said. "It's the religion of the Second Chance."

Then he set the hymnals on the counter and turned to offer Ian a beatific smile. Ian thought he had never seen anyone so absolutely at peace.

"I don't understand," his mother said.

"What's to understand? It's simple," Ian told her. "What you mean is, you don't approve."

"Well, of course she doesn't approve," his father said. "Neither one of us approves. No one in his right mind would approve. Here you are, attending a perfectly decent college which you barely got into by the skin of your teeth, incidentally; you've had no complaints about the place that your mother or I are aware of; you're due back this Sunday evening to begin your second semester and what do you up and tell us? You're dropping out."

"I'm taking a leave of absence," Ian said.

They were sitting in the dining room late Friday night— much too late to have only then finished supper, but Daphne had developed an earache and what with one thing and another it had somehow got to be nine p.m. before they'd put the children in bed. Now Bee, having risen to clear the table, sank back into her chair. Doug shoved his plate away and leaned his elbows on the table. "Just tell me this," he said to Ian. "How long do you expect this leave of absence to last?"

"Oh, maybe till Daphne's in first grade. Or kindergarten, at least," Ian said.

"Daphne? What's Daphne got to do with it?"

"The reason I'm taking a leave is to help Mom raise the kids."

"Me?" his mother cried. "I'm not raising those children! We're looking for a guardian! First we'll find Lucy's people and then I know there'll be someone, some young couple maybe who would just love to—"

"Mom," Ian said. "You know the chances of that are getting slimmer all the time."

"I know nothing of the sort! Or an aunt, maybe, or—"

Doug said, "Well, he's got a point, Bee. You've been running yourself ragged with those kids."

Contrarily, Ian felt a pinch of alarm. Would his father really let him go through with this?

His mother said, "And anyway, how about the draft? You'll be drafted the minute you leave school."

"If I am, I am," Ian told her, "but I don't think I will be. I think God will take care of that."

"Who?"

"And I do plan to pay my own way," he said. "I've already found a job."

"Doing what?" his father asked. "Moving poor folks' furniture?"

"*Building* furniture."

They peered at him.

"I've made arrangements with this cabinetmaker," Ian said. "I've seen him at work and I asked if I could be his apprentice."

Student, was the way he'd finally put it. Having sought out the cabinetmaker in that apartment full of china crates and moth-balls, he had plunged into the subject of apprenticeship only to be met with a baffled stare. The man had sat back on his heels and studied Ian's lips. "Apprentice," Ian had repeated, enunciating carefully. "Pupil."

"People?" the man had asked. Two furrows stitched themselves across his leathery forehead.

"I already have some experience," Ian said. "I used to help my father in the basement. I know I could build a kitchen cabinet."

"I dislike kitchens," the man said harshly.

For a moment, Ian thought he still hadn't made himself clear. But the man went on: "They're junk. See this hinge." He pointed to it—an ornately curlicued piece of black metal, dimpled all over with artificial hammer marks. "My real work is furniture," he said.

"Fine," Ian told him. What did he care? Kitchen cabinets, furniture, it was all the same to him: inanimate objects. Something he could deal with that he couldn't mess up. Or if he did mess up, it was possible to repair the damage.

"I have a workshop. I make things I like," the man said. He spoke like anyone else except for a certain insistence of tone, a thickness in the consonants, as if he had a cold. "These kitchens, they're just for the money."

"That's okay! That's fine! And as for money," Ian said, "you could pay me minimum wage. Or lower, to start with, because I'm just an apprentice. Student," he added, for he saw now that it was the uncommon word "apprentice" that had given trouble. "And any time you have to do a kitchen, you could send me instead."

He knew he had a hope, then. He could tell by the wistful, visionary look that slowly dawned in the man's gray eyes.

But were his parents impressed with Ian's initiative? No. They just sat there blankly. "It's not brute labor, after all," he told them. "It's a craft! It's like an art."

"Ian," his father said, "if you're busy learning this . . . art, how will you help with the kids?"

"I'll work out a schedule with my boss," Ian said. "Also there's this church that's going to pitch in."

"This what?"

"Church."

They tilted their heads.

"There's this . . . it's kind of hard to explain," he said. "This church sort of place on York Road, see, that believes you have to really do something practical to atone for your, shall we call them, sins. And if you agree to that, they'll pitch in. You can sign up on a bulletin board—the hours you need help, the hours you've got free to help others—"

"What in the name of God . . . ?" Bee asked.

"Well, that's just it," Ian said. "I mean, I don't want to sound corny or anything but it *is* in the name of God. 'Let us not love in—' what—'in just words or in tongue, but in—' "

"Ian, have you fallen into the hands of some *sect?*" his father asked.

"No, I haven't," Ian said. "I have merely discovered a church that makes sense to me, the same as Dober Street Presbyterian makes sense to you and Mom."

"Dober Street didn't ask us to abandon our educations," his mother told him. "Of course we have nothing against religion; we raised all of you children to be Christians. But *our* church never asked us to abandon our entire way of life."

"Well, maybe it should have," Ian said.

His parents looked at each other.

His mother said, "I don't believe this. I do not believe it. No matter how long I've been a mother, it seems my children can still come up with something new and unexpected to do to me."

"I'm not doing this to *you!* Why does everything have to relate to *you* all the time? It's for me, can't you get that into your head? It's something I have to do for myself, to be forgiven."

"Forgiven what, Ian?" his father asked.

Ian swallowed.

"You're nineteen years old, son. You're a fine, considerate, upstanding human being. What sin could you possibly be guilty of that would require you to uproot your whole existence?"

Reverend Emmett had said Ian would have to tell them. He'd

said that was the only way. Ian had tried to explain how much it would hurt them, but Reverend Emmett had held firm. Sometimes a wound must be scraped out before it can heal, he had said.

Ian said, "I'm the one who caused Danny to die. He drove into that wall on purpose."

Nobody spoke. His mother's face was white, almost flinty.

"I told him Lucy was, um, not faithful," he said.

He had thought there would be questions. He had assumed they would ask for details, pull the single strand he'd handed them till the whole ugly story came tumbling out. But they just sat silent, staring at him.

"I'm sorry!" he cried. "I'm *really* sorry!"

His mother moved her lips, which seemed unusually wrinkled. No sound emerged.

After a while, he rose awkwardly and left the table. He paused in the dining room doorway, just in case they wanted to call him back. But they didn't. He crossed the hall and started up the stairs.

For the first time it occurred to him that there was something steely and inhuman to this religion business. Had Reverend Emmett taken fully into account the lonely thud of his sneakers on the steps, the shattered, splintered air he left behind him?

The little lamp on his desk gave off just enough light so it wouldn't wake Daphne. He leaned over the crib to check on her. She had a feverish smell that reminded him of a sour dishcloth. He straightened her blanket, and then he crossed to the bureau and looked in the mirror that hung above it. Back-lit, he was nothing but a silhouette. He saw himself suddenly as the figure he had feared in his childhood, the intruder who lurked beneath his bed so he had to take a running leap from the doorway every night. He turned aside sharply and picked up the mail his mother had set out for him: a *Playboy* magazine, an advertisement for a record club, a postcard from his roommate. The magazine and the ad he dropped into the wastebasket. The postcard showed a wild-haired woman barely covered by a white fur dress that hung in strategic zigzags around her thighs. (*SHE-WOLVES OF ANT-ARCTICA! In ViviColor!* the legend read.) *Dear Ian, How do you like my Christmas card? Better late than never. Kind of boring here at home, no Ian and Cicely across the room oh-so-silently hanky-panking* . . . He winced and dropped the card on top of the magazine. It made a whiskery sound as it landed.

He saw that he was beginning from scratch, from the very ground level, as low as he could get. It was a satisfaction, really.

That night he dreamed he was carrying a cardboard moving carton for Sid 'n' Ed. It held books or something; it weighed a ton. "Here," Danny said, "let me help you," and he took one end and started backing down the steps with it. And all the while he and Ian smiled into each other's eyes.

It was the last such dream Ian would ever have of Danny, although of course he didn't know that at the time. At the time he woke clenched and anxious, and all he could think of for comfort was the hymn they had sung in the Church of the Second Chance. "Leaning," they sang, "leaning, leaning on the everlasting arms . . ." Gradually he drifted loose, giving himself over to God. He rested all his weight on God, trustfully, serenely, the way his roommate used to rest in his chair that resembled the palm of a hand.

4

Famous
Rainbows

Holy Roller, their grandma called it. Holy Roller Bible Camp.
She shut a cupboard door and told Thomas, "If you all went to
real camp instead of Holy Roller, you wouldn't have to get up
at the crack of dawn every day. And I wouldn't be standing here
half asleep trying to fix you some breakfast."

But it wasn't the crack of dawn. Hot yellow bands of sunshine
stretched across the linoleum. And she didn't look half asleep,
either. She already had her hair combed, fluffed around her face
in a curly gray shower-cap shape. She was wearing the blouse
Thomas liked best, the one printed like a newspaper page, and
brown knit slacks stretched out in front by the cozy ball of her
stomach.

One of the words on her blouse was VICTORY. Another was

DISASTER. Thomas hadn't even started second grade yet but he was able to read nearly every word you showed him.

"If you all went to Camp Cottontail like the Parker children you wouldn't have to leave till nine a.m.," his grandma said, inching around the table with a stack of cereal bowls. "An air-conditioned bus would pick you up at the doorstep. But oh, no. *Oh*, no. That's too simple for your uncle Ian. Let's not do it the easy way, your uncle Ian says."

What Ian had really said was, "Camp Cottontail costs eighty dollars for a two-week session." Thomas had heard the whole argument. "Eighty dollars per child! Do you realize what that comes to?"

"Maybe Dad could make a bit extra teaching summer school," their grandma had told him.

"Dream on, Mom. You really think I'd let him do that? Also, Camp Cottontail doesn't take three-year-olds. Daphne would be home all day with little old *you*."

That was what had settled it. Their grandma had the arthritis in her knees and hips and sometimes now in her hands, and chasing after Daphne was too much for her. Daphne just did her in, Grandma always said. Dearly though she loved her.

She shook Cheerios into Thomas's bowl and then turned toward the stairs. "Agatha!" she called. "Agatha, are you up?"

No answer. She sighed and poured milk on top of the Cheerios. "You get started on these and I'll go give her a nudge," she told Thomas. She walked stiffly out of the kitchen, calling, "Rise and shine, Agatha!"

Thomas laid his spoon flat on top of his cereal and watched it fill with milk and then sink.

Now here came his grandpa and Ian, with Daphne just behind. Ian wore his work clothes—faded jeans and a T-shirt, his white cloth carpenter cap turned around backwards like a baseball catcher's. (Grandma just despaired when her men kept their hats on in the house.) He'd dressed Daphne in her new pink shorts set, and she was pulling the toy plastic lawn mower that made colored balls pop up when the wheels turned.

"The way I figure it," Ian was saying, "we'd be better off moving the whole operation to someplace where the lumber could be stored in the same building. But Mr. Brant likes the shop where it is. So I'm going to need the car all day unless you . . ."

Thomas stopped listening and took a mouthful of cereal. He watched Daphne walk around and around Ian's legs, with the lawn mower bobbling behind her. "This is what I'm bringing to Sharing Hour," she announced, but Thomas was the only one who heard her. "Ian? This is what I'm—"

"You should bring something fancier," Thomas told her.

"No! I'm bringing this!"

"Remember yesterday, what Mindy brought?"

Mindy had brought an Egyptian beetle from about a million years ago, pale blue-green like old rain spouts. But Daphne said, "I don't care."

"*Lots* of people have plastic lawn mowers," Thomas told her.

She pretended not to hear and walked in tighter and tighter circles around Ian's blue denim legs.

Once Daphne had her mind made up, nothing could change it. Everyone always joked about that. But Thomas worried she would look dumb in front of Bible camp. It was such a small camp that all the children were jumbled together, the three-year-olds in with the seven-year-olds like Thomas and even Agatha's age, the ten-year-olds; even ten-year-old Dermott Kyle. Dermott Kyle would be sure to laugh at her. Thomas watched her round-nosed white sandals taking tiny steps and he started getting angry at her just thinking about it.

Then Ian bent over and scooped her up, lawn mower and all. He said, "What's your breakfast order, Miss Daph?" and she giggled and told him, "Cinnamon toast."

That Daphne was too ignorant to worry.

When Agatha came downstairs she looked puffy-eyed and dazed. She never woke up easily. Their grandma hobbled around her, trying to get her going—pushing the Cheerios box across the table to her and offering other kinds when Agatha shook her head. "Cornflakes? Raisin bran?" she said. Agatha rested her chin on her fist and her eyes started slowly, slowly drooping shut. "Agatha, *don't* go back to sleep."

"She'll be fine once she hits fresh air," Ian said. He was standing by the toaster, waiting for Daphne's toast to pop up. He'd set Daphne on the counter next to him where she swung her feet and banged her heels against the cupboard doors beneath her.

"She'd be even finer if she could sleep till a decent hour," their grandma told him. "Why, they're having to get up earlier in summer than in winter! Poor child can barely keep her eyes propped open."

"She ought to be in Camp Cottontail," their grandpa said suddenly. Everyone had forgotten about him. He was scrambling himself some eggs at the stove. "Camp Cottontail comes to the house for them about nine o'clock or so; I've seen the bus in the neighborhood."

"Wasn't I just saying that? While Holy Roller, on the other hand—"

"It's not Holy Roller, Mom. Please," Ian told her. "It's Camp Second Chance. And it's sponsored by my church and it's free of charge. Not to mention it offers the kids a little grounding for their lives."

Their grandma looked up at the ceiling and let out a long, noisy breath.

"When I was seventeen," their grandpa said from the stove, "I volunteered to be a counselor at my church's camp out in western Maryland. That's because I was in love with this girl who taught archery there. Marie, her name was. I can see her still. She wore this leather cuff on her wrist so the bowstring wouldn't thwack her. Every night I prayed and prayed for her to love me back. I said, 'God, if you'll do this one thing for me I'll believe in you forever and I'll never ask another favor.' But she preferred the lifeguard and they started going out together. After that, why, me and God just never have been that chummy."

"God and I," Grandma murmured automatically.

we undertake is God's work; I am an arrow shot by God to do His handiwork."

He did look something like an arrow: straight and smooth, a sharp cowlick sticking up on the crown of his head.

"What exactly *is* your work?" Ian asked him, hoping to change the subject.

"I'm a private detective."

This was so unexpected that Ian laughed. Eli scowled. "What's funny about that?" he said.

"Detective?" Ian said. "You mean, like solving murders and mysteries and such?"

"Well, it's more like tailing husbands to motel rooms. But that's the Lord's business too! Believe me."

"If you say so," Ian told him.

"What do you do, brother?"

"I'm a carpenter," Ian said.

"Our Savior was a carpenter."

"Well, yes."

"Nothing to be ashamed of."

"Who said I was ashamed?"

"Those your kids you came with?"

"Yes."

"You look kind of young to have kids that old."

"Really I'm just their uncle," Ian said. "My parents and I take care of them."

"I would've thought you were nothing but a college boy."

"No, no."

"You married?"

"No."

"A bachelor."

"Well, yes. A . . . bachelor," Ian said.

Eli bent over a hinge again. Ian watched for a minute and then turned back to his ladder.

But the next time he brought down a shutter, he said, "So you've never found a missing person, or anything like that."

"Depends on what you call missing," Eli said. "Sure, I've found a few husbands here and there. Usually they're just staying with a girlfriend, though, that everybody except their wives knows the name and address of."

"I see," Ian said.

He leaned the shutter against a sawhorse. He studied it. Not looking at Eli, he said, "Say a person had been missing a long time. Five or six years, say. Maybe seven or eight. Would the trail be too cold for you to follow?"

"What? Naw," Eli said. "Bound to be *something* he left behind. People are so messy. That's been my experience. People leave so much litter wherever they go to."

He rotated one forearm and examined the inside of his wrist. A dribble of dusty blood ran downward from his palm. "Somebody special you had in mind?" he asked.

"Not really," Ian said.

He brushed a dead leaf from a louver. He cleared his throat. He said, "Those kids I'm taking care of: their father is missing, I guess you could say. The father of the older two."

"Is that so," Eli said. "Ducking his child support, huh?"

"Child support? Oh. Right," Ian said.

"Boy, I hate those child-support guys," Eli said. "Or, no, not hate. Forget hate. The Bible cautions us not to hate. But I . . . pity them, yes, I surely do pity those child-support guys. You'd never get *me* to raise one of them's kids."

"Oh, they're really like my own now," Ian said.

"Even so! Here you are sitting home with three young ones and he's off enjoying his self."

"I don't mind," Ian said.

He didn't want to go into the whole story. In fact, he couldn't remember now why he'd brought it up in the first place.

He was supervising the children's homework at the kitchen table when he heard a wailing sound outdoors. He said, "Was that a baby?"

No one answered. They were too busy arguing. Thomas was telling Daphne that when *he* was in third grade, a plain old wooden pencil had been good enough for him. Daphne had no business, he said, swiping his personal ballpoint pen. Daphne said, "Maybe what *you* wrote in third grade wasn't worth a pen." Then Agatha complained they'd made her lose her train of thought. Thanks to them, she would have to start this whole equation over again.

"Was that a baby crying?" Ian asked.

They barely paused.

"Hey," Thomas said to the others. "Want to hear something disgusting?"

"No, what?"

Ian crossed the kitchen and opened the screen door. It was light enough still so he could make out the clothesline poles and the azalea bushes, and the stockade fence that separated the backyard from the alley.

"In science class, my teacher? Mr. Pratt?" Thomas said. "He stands at the blackboard, he tells us, 'By the time I've finished teaching this lesson, microscopic portions of my mouth will be *all over this room.*' "

"Eeuw!" Daphne and Agatha said.

Just inside the gate, which had not been completely closed in years, sat a minuscule patch of darkness, a denser black than the fence posts. This patch stirred and glinted in some way and uttered another thin wail.

"Kitty-kitty?" Ian called.

He stepped outside, shutting the screen door behind him. Yes, it was definitely a cat. When he approached, it teetered on the brink of leaving but finally stood its ground. He bent to pat its head. He could feel the narrow skull beneath fur so soft that it made almost no impression on his fingertips.

"Where's your owner, little cat?" he asked.

But he thought he knew the answer to that. There wasn't any tag or collar, and when he ran a hand down its body he could count the ribs. It staggered weakly beneath his touch, then braced itself and started purring in a rusty, unpracticed way, pressing its small face into the cup of his palm.

As it happened, the Bedloes had no pets at that particular moment. They had never replaced Beastie, and the latest of their cats had disappeared a few months ago. So this new little cat had come to the right people. Ian let it spend a few minutes getting used to him, and then he picked it up and carried it back inside the house. It clung to him with needle claws, tense but still conscientiously purring. "See what I found in the alley," he told the children.

"Oh, look!" Daphne cried, slipping out of her chair. "Can I hold it, Ian? Can I keep it?"

"If no one comes to claim it," Ian said, handing it over.

In the light he saw that the cat was black from head to foot, and not much more than half grown. Its eyes had changed to green already but its face was still the triangular, top-heavy face of a kitten. Thomas was lifting its spindly tail to see what sex it was, but the cat objected to that and climbed higher on Daphne's shoulder. "Ouch!" Daphne squawked. "Thomas, quit! See what you made it do?"

"It's a girl, I think," Thomas announced.

"Leave her alone, Thomas!"

"She's not just yours, Daphne," Agatha said. She had risen too and was scratching the cat behind its ears.

"She is so mine! Ian said so! You're mine, mine, mine, you little sweetums," Daphne said, nuzzling the cat's nose with her own. "Oh, what kind of monstrous, mean person would just ditch you and drive off?"

All of a sudden Ian had an image of Agatha, Thomas, and Daphne huddled in a ditch by the side of a road. They were hanging onto each other and their eyes were wide and fearful. And far in the distance, almost out of sight, Ian's car was vanishing around a curve.

But then immediately afterward, he felt such a deep sense of loss that it made his breath catch.

. . .

His mother was truly disabled now. Oh, she still hobbled from room to room, she still insisted on standing over the stove and creeping behind the dust mop, but the arthritis had seized up her hands and the finer motions of day-to-day life were beyond her. Folding the laundry, driving the car, buttoning Daphne's dress down the back—all that was left to Ian and his father. And Ian's father was not much help. Any task he began seemed to end in, "How the dickens . . . ?" and "Ian, can you come here a minute?" In the old days Claudia had stopped by once or twice a week to see what needed doing, but she had moved to Pittsburgh when Macy found a better job; and first they'd returned for holidays but now they didn't even do that very often.

Meanwhile, these children were a full-time occupation. They were good children, bright children; they did well in school and never got in serious trouble. But even nonserious trouble could consume a great deal of energy, Ian had learned. Agatha, for instance, was suffering all the miseries of adolescence. Every morning she set off for school alone and friendless—the earnest, pale, studious kind of girl Ian had ignored when he himself was her age, but now he cursed those callow high-school kids who couldn't see how special she was, how intelligent and witty and perceptive. Thomas, on the other hand, had too *many* friends. Tall and graceful, his voice already cracking and a shadow darkening his upper lip, he was more interested in socializing than in schoolwork, and one or another of the Bedloes was always having to attend parent-teacher conferences—most often Ian, it seemed.

As for Daphne, she wound through life sparkling at everyone and lowering her long black lashes over stunning blue-black eyes; but any time you crossed her there was hell to pay. She was *fierce*, that Daphne. "I think she had a difficult infancy," Ian was always explaining. "She's really a good kid, believe me. She just feels she's got to fend for herself," he told a teacher. Yet another teacher. At yet another parent-teacher conference. (His second of the year, and school had been in session only ten days.)

Cicely was living out in California now with a folk guitarist. Pig Benson's family had moved away while he was in the army. Andrew was in graduate school at Tulane. And anyhow, the last time Andrew came home it turned out he and Ian didn't have much to talk about. At one point Andrew had referred to the "goddamned holiday traffic," and then reddened and said, "Sorry," so Ian knew he'd heard about Second Chance from someone. And then Ian had to take Daphne for her booster shots, and that was that. Andrew had not suggested getting together again.

Bachelor. What a dashing word. Ian the bachelor. He would live in an apartment all his own. (A bachelor pad.) He'd have friends his own age dropping by to visit. Young women going out with him. And no one trailing behind to ask, "But how about *us*? Who will see to us? Who will find our socks for us and help with our history project?"

At work, he was putting the final touches on a drop-front desk. He was rubbing linseed oil into the wood, while Bert, one of the new men, worked on a bureau across the room.

Their kitchen-cabinet days were over, thank heaven. Now rich young couples from Bolton Hill showed up at Mr. Brant's shop to commission one-of-a-kind furniture: bookcases custom-fitted to Bolton Hill's high ceilings, stand-up desks made to measure, and Shaker-looking benches. Everything was built the old way, with splines and rabbets and lap joints, no nails, no stains or plastic finishes. Orders were backed up a year or more and they'd had to hire three new employees.

You'd think this would delight Mr. Brant, but he remained as morose as always. Or was that only his deafness? No, because whenever his wife dropped by—a much younger woman who'd been deaf from birth, unlike Mr. Brant—she would sign to him with flying fingers, her face lighting up and clouding over to go with what she said; and Ian could see she lived a life as full and talkative as any hearing person's. Mr. Brant would watch her without altering his expression, and then he would make a few signs of his own—clumsy, blunt signs, stiff-thumbed. Ian wondered how on earth they had courted. What could Mr. Brant have said that would win such a woman's heart? When Mrs. Brant watched his hands, her eyes grew very intent and focused and all the animation left her. Ian had the feeling her husband was somehow dampening her enthusiasm, but maybe it only seemed that way.

One of the new employees was Mrs. Brant's niece, a rosy, bosomy girl named Jeannie who'd dropped out of college to do something more real. (They were seeing a lot of that nowadays.) Jeannie said Mrs. Brant was a regular social butterfly. She said Mrs. Brant had dozens of friends who'd gone to Gallaudet with her, and they would sit around her kitchen talking away a mile a minute, using their special sign language with lots of inside jokes and dirty words; but her husband had come late to sign and could barely manage such basics as "Serve supper" and "Mail letter" (like Tonto, Jeannie said), so of course he was left in the dust. He was neither fish nor fowl, Jeannie said. This made Ian feel fonder of the man. He had long ago given up all hope of befriending him, or of seeing any hint of emotion in that handsome, leathery face; but now he regretted dismissing him so easily. "He must be awfully lonesome," he told Jeannie, "watching his wife enjoy herself with her friends."

"Oh, he doesn't care," Jeannie said. "He just stomps off to his garden. None of us can figure why she married him. Maybe it was sex. I do think he's kind of sexy, don't you?"

Jeannie often talked that way. She made Ian feel uncomfortable. Several times she had suggested they go out together some evening, and although he did find her attractive, with her streaming hair and bouncy peasant blouses, he always gave some excuse.

This afternoon she was helping Bert with his bureau. (She didn't know enough yet to be entrusted with a piece all her own.) Her job was to attach the drawer knobs—perfectly plain beechwood cylinders—but she kept leaving them to come over and talk to Ian. "Pretty," she said of the desk. Then, without a pause, "You like nature, Ian?"

"Nature? Sure."

"Me and some friends are taking a picnic lunch to Loch Raven this Sunday. Want to come?"

"Well, I have church on Sundays," Ian told her.

"Church," she said. She rocked back on the heels of her moccasins. "But how about *after* church?" she said. "We wouldn't be leaving till one or so."

"Oh, uh, there's my nephew and nieces, too," Ian said. "I sort of have to keep an eye on them on weekends."

"Why can't their parents do that?"

"Their parents are dead."

"Their grandparents, then," she said, instantly readjusting.

"My mother's got arthritis and my dad is kind of tied up."

"Or the other grandparents! Or other aunts and uncles! Or baby-sitters! Or can't the older ones watch the younger ones? Or maybe you could call the mothers of some of their school friends and see if—"

"It's kind of involved," Ian said. He was surprised at the number of options that could be produced at such short notice. "I guess I'd just better say no," he told her.

"Christ," she said, "what a drag. Why, even chain gangs get their Sundays off."

Then Mr. Brant called, "Jeannie!" He towered over the bureau, glaring in her direction, and she said, "Oops! Gotta go."

She skipped away, a juicy morsel of a girl, and Ian noticed how her long hair swung against the tight-packed seat of her jeans.

He had made it up about the children, of course. They were well past the stage when they needed sitters. But somehow he began to believe his own alibi, and as he watched her he thought, *Right! Even chain gangs,* he thought, *are allowed a little time to themselves.*

Well, no one had ever said this would be easy.

But then why didn't he feel forgiven? Why didn't he, after all these years of penance, feel that God had forgiven him?

The little black cat settled in immediately. She was very polite and clean, with a smell like new woolen yarn, and she tolerated any amount of petting. Daphne named her Honeybunch. Thomas named her Alexandra. Any time one would call her, the other would call louder. "Here, Honeybunch." "No, *Alexandra!* Here, Alexandra, you know who you love best." Agatha stayed out of it. She was abstracted all that weekend, moping because a classmate had thrown a party without inviting her. The reason Ian knew this was that Thomas announced it, cruelly, during Saturday night supper. Agatha had told Thomas he was piggish to chew with his mouth open, and Thomas said, "Well, at least I don't have to buy my clothes in the Chubbette department. At least I'm not so fat that Missy Perkins wouldn't ask me to her slumber party!" Then Agatha threw down her napkin and bolted from the table, and Daphne said, in a satisfied tone, "You're a meanie, Thomas."

"Am not."

"Are so."

"She started it."

"Did not."

"Did so."

"Quit that," Ian said. "Both of you may be excused."

"Why do *I* have to go when he's the one who—"

"You're excused, I said."

They left, grumbling under their breaths as they moved into the living room.

Supper was more or less finished, anyhow. Ian's father had

already pushed away his plate and tilted back in his chair, and his mother was merely toying with her dessert. She hadn't taken a bite in the last five minutes; she was deep in one of her blow-by-blow household sagas, and it seemed she would never get around to eating her last half-globe of canned peach.

"So there I was in the basement," she said, "looking at all this water full of let's-not-discuss-it, and the man pulled a kind of zippery tube from his machine and twined it down the . . ."

Ian started thinking about the comics. It was childish of him, he knew, but one thing he really enjoyed at the end of every day was reading "Peanuts" in the *Evening Sun*. It made a kind of oasis—that tiny, friendly world where everybody was so quaint and earnest and reflective. But what with Good Works, and the weekly grocery trip, and shopping for the kids' new gym shoes, he hadn't had a chance at the paper yet; and now he could hear the others mauling it in the living room. By the time he got hold of it all the pages would be disarranged and crumpled.

"The total bill came to sixty dollars," his mother was saying. "I consider that cheap, in view of what the man had to deal with. When he was done he had me look down the floor drain. Big dark echoey floor drain. 'Hear that?' he said, and I said, 'Hear what?' He said, 'All along the line, your neighbors flushing their toilets. First one here and then one far, far away over there,' he said, 'all connected by this network of pipes.' 'Well, fine,' I said, 'but left to my own devices I believe I could manage to live out my life *not* hearing, thank you very much.' "

In the living room, quarrelsome voices climbed over each other and Ian caught the sound of paper tearing. They were demolishing "Peanuts," he was certain. He sighed.

Suppose, he thought suddenly, his boyhood self was to walk into the scene at this moment. Suppose he was offered a glimpse of how he had turned out: twenty-six years old and still living with his parents, tending someone else's children, obsessed with the evening comics. *Huh?* he'd say. *Why, what has happened here? What has become of me? How in heaven's name did things ever get to this state?*

"Give me one good reason I should have to go to church," Agatha said on Sunday morning. "It's hypocritical to go! I'm not a believer."

"You can go to Grandma and Grandpa's church if you prefer," Ian told her.

"Listen carefully, Ian, I'll only say this one more time: *I am not a believer.*"

He wrapped an elastic around Daphne's ponytail. "How about this," he said. "You attend till you're eighteen, and then you stop. That way, I won't have to feel guilty you didn't get the proper foundation."

"You don't have to feel guilty even now," Agatha told him. "I absolve you, Ian."

He drew back slightly. Absolve?

"Maybe she could go to Mary McQueen," Daphne suggested.

Agatha said, "Mary Our Queen is for Catholics, stupid."

"Agatha, don't call her stupid. Let's get moving. Thomas is already downstairs."

They descended to the living room, Daphne clattering in the patent leather Mary Janes she liked to wear to church. The sound of Sunday morning, Ian thought. He told his parents, "We're off."

"Oh, all right, dear," his mother said. She and his father were reading the paper on the couch.

"Take that business of the fig tree," Agatha said as she let the front door slam behind her. "Jesus cursing the fig tree."

"Where's Thomas?"

"Here I am," Thomas said from the porch swing.

"Let's go, then."

"Jesus decides he wants figs," Agatha said. "Of course, it's not fig *season*, but Jesus wants figs anyhow. So up he walks to this fig tree, but naturally all he finds is leaves. And what does he do? Puts a curse on the poor little tree."

"No!" Daphne breathed. Evidently she hadn't heard about this before.

"Next thing you know, the tree's withered and died."

"No."

Ian knew that Agatha was just passing through a stage, but even so he minded, a bit. Over the years he had come to view Jesus very personally. The most trite and sentimental Sunday School portrait could send a flash of feeling through him, as if Jesus were . . . oh, one of those older boys he used to admire when he was small, someone he'd watched from a distance and grown to know and love without ever daring to engage in conversation.

Also, Agatha was seeding doubts in the other two.

"Doesn't that seem petty to you?" she was asking Daphne. "I mean, doesn't it seem unreasonable? If *we* behaved like that, we'd be sent to our rooms to think it over."

"Agatha," Ian said, "there's a great deal in the Bible that's simply beyond our understanding."

"Beyond yours, maybe," Agatha said. She told Daphne, "Or Noah's Ark: how about that? God kills off all the sinners in a mammoth rainstorm. 'Gotcha!' he says, and he's enjoying it, you know he is, or otherwise he'd have sent a few sample rains ahead of time so they could mend their ways."

Picture how they must look from outside, Ian thought. A cleaned and pressed little family walking together to church, discussing matters of theology. Perfect.

From outside.

"Or Abraham and Isaac. That one *really* ticks me off. God asks Abraham to kill his own son. And Abraham says, 'Okay.' Can you believe it? And then at the very last minute God says, 'Only testing. Ha-ha.' Boy, I'd like to know what Isaac thought. All the rest of his life, any time his father so much as looked in his direction Isaac would think—"

Ian said, "Agatha, it's very bad manners to criticize other people's religion."

"It's very bad manners to force your own religion on them, too," Agatha told him. "Shoot, it's very *unconstitutional*. To make me go to church when I don't want to."

"Well, you're right," Ian said.

"Huh?"

"You're right, I shouldn't have done it."

By now, they had stopped walking. Agatha peered at him. She said, "So can I leave now?"

"You can leave."

She stood there a moment longer. The other two watched with interest. "Okay," she said finally. "Bye."

"Bye."

She turned and set off toward home.

But without her it seemed so quiet. He missed her firm, opinionated voice and that little trick she had of varying her tone to quote each person's remarks. No matter how imaginary those remarks might be.

"I the Lord thy God am a jealous God," Reverend Emmett read from Exodus, and Ian could almost hear Agatha beside him: "Any time *we* act jealous, people have a fit." He shook the thought away. He bowed lower in his seat, propping his forehead on two fingers. Next to him, Daphne tore a tiny corner off a page of her hymnal and placed it on her tongue. Thomas was sitting behind them with Kenny Larson and his family. A fly was crawling up the front counter.

Reverend Emmett called for a hymn: "Blessed Assurance." The congregation rose to sing, standing shoulder to shoulder. Everyone here was familiar to Ian. Or at least, semifamiliar. (Eli Everjohn and his wife were sitting with Sister Bertha, and Mrs. Jordan had brought her cousin.) "This is my story," they sang, "this is my song . . ." Ian put an arm around Daphne and she nestled against him as she sang, her voice incongruously husky for such a little girl.

The sermon was on the Sugar Rule. Recently a committee had approached Reverend Emmett suggesting that the rule be dropped. It was just so complicated, they said. Face it, they were eating sugar every day of their lives, one way or another. Even peanut butter contained sugar if you bought it from a supermarket. Reverend Emmett had told them he would meditate on the issue and report his conclusions. What he said this morning—pacing behind the counter, running his long fingers through his forelock—was that the Sugar Rule was *supposed* to be complicated. "Like error itself," he said, "sugar creeps in the cracks. You tell yourself you didn't realize, you were subject to circumstance, you forgot to read the list of ingredients and anyhow, it's everywhere and it can't be helped. Isn't that significant? It's not that you'll be damned forever if you take a grain of sugar; nobody says that. Sugar is merely a distraction, not a sin. But I feel it's important to keep the rule because of what it stands for: the need for eternal watchfulness."

The children—those who were listening—sent each other disappointed grimaces, but Ian didn't really care that much. The Sugar Rule was a minor inconvenience, at most. So was the Coffee Rule; so was the Alcohol Rule. The difficult one was the Unmarried Sex Rule. "How can something be right one day and wrong the next?" Cicely had asked him. "And what's done is done, anyway, and can't be undone, right?"

He had said, "If I thought that, I wouldn't be able to go on living." Then he'd told her he wanted them to get married.

"Married!" Cicely had cried. "Married, at our age! I haven't seen the world yet! I haven't had any fun!"

He covered his eyes with his hand.

In his daydreams, he walked into services one morning and found a lovely, golden-haired girl sitting in the row just ahead. She would be so intent on the sermon that she wouldn't even look his way; she had grown up in a religion very much like this

one, it turned out, and believed with all her heart. After the
Benediction Ian introduced himself, and she looked shy and
pleased. They had the most proper courtship, but he could tell
she felt the same way he did. They would marry at Second
Chance with Reverend Emmett officiating. She would love the
three children as much as if they were hers and stay home forever
after to tend them. The Church Maiden, Ian called her in his
mind. He never entered this building without scanning the rows
for the Church Maiden.

After the sermon came Amending. "Does somebody want to
stand up?" Reverend Emmett asked. But standing up was for
serious sins, where you confessed to the whole congregation and
discussed in public all possible methods of atonement. Evidently
none of them had strayed so grievously during this past week.
"Well, then," Reverend Emmett said, smiling, "we'll amend in
private," and they bowed their heads and whispered their mistakes
to themselves. Ian caught snatches of "lied to my husband" and
"slapped my daughter" and "drank part of a beer with my boss."
"Thursday I stole my sister's new bra and wore it to gym class,"
Daphne said, startling Ian, but of course he should not have been
listening. He averted his face from her and whispered, "I was
snappish with the children three different times. Four. And I
told Mr. Brant I was sick with the flu when really I just wanted
a day off."

Unlike the other denominations Ian knew of, this one had
nothing against sinning in your thoughts. To think a sinful
thought and not act upon it was to practice righteousness, Reverend Emmett said—almost as much righteousness as not thinking the thought in the first place. Jesus must have been misquoted
on that business about committing adultery in your heart. So Ian
left unspoken what troubled him the most:

I've been atoning and atoning, and sometimes lately I've hated
God for taking so long to forgive me. Some days I feel I'm speaking
into a dead telephone. My words are knocking against a blank
wall. Nothing comes back to show I've been heard.

"Let it vanish now from our souls, Lord. In Jesus' name, amen," Reverend Emmett said. He looked radiant. Whatever had weighed on his own soul (for his lips had moved with the others', this morning) had obviously been lifted from him.

They sang "Sweet Hour of Prayer," in a tone that struck Ian as lingering and regretful. Then Reverend Emmett gave the Benediction, and they were free to go. Daphne shot off to join a friend. Ian wove his way through the other members' greetings. He answered several inquiries about his mother's arthritis, and politely refused Mrs. Jordan's offer of a ride home. (She drove like a maniac.) Near the door, Eli Everjohn stood awkwardly by in a brilliant blue suit while his wife talked with Sister Myra. "Morning, Brother Eli," Ian said. He started to edge past him, but Eli, who must have been feeling left out, brightened and said, "Why, hey there! Hey!"

"Enjoy the service?" Ian asked.

"Oh, I'm sure your pastor means well," Eli said. "But forbidding ordinary white sugar, and then allowing your young folks to listen to rock-and-roll music! Seems like to me he's got his priorities mixed up. I don't know that I hold with this Amending business, either. Awful close to Roman Catholic, if you ask me."

"Ah, well, it's a matter of opinion, I guess."

"No, Brother Ian, it is *not* a matter of opinion. Goodness! What a notion."

That more or less finished the conversation, Ian figured. He gave up and raised a hand amiably in farewell. But then he paused and turned back. "Brother Eli?" he said. "I wonder. Do you think you could locate a missing person for me?"

"Why, I'll do my best," Eli told him.

He didn't seem at all surprised by the question. It was Ian who was surprised.

"His name was Tom Dean," he told Eli. "Thomas Dean, Senior. He was married to my sister-in-law before she married my brother, and he's the only one who might be able to tell us who my sister-in-law's family was."

He and Eli sat on the couch in Sister Bertha's living room. No doubt Sister Bertha was wondering what business Ian could possibly have here, but she stayed out of sight, ostentatiously rattling pans in the kitchen and talking to her daughter. Her house was a ranch house with rooms that all flowed together, and Ian distinctly heard her discussing someone named Netta who had suffered a terrible grease fire.

"I don't know where Tom Dean grew up," Ian said, "but sometime in the spring of 'sixty-five he wrote to Lucy from Cheyenne, Wyoming. Or maybe he phoned; I'm not sure. *Somehow* he got in touch, asking her to send him his things."

"How long had they been divorced?" Eli said.

"I don't know. The kids were still small, though. It can't have been too long."

"And what state was this divorce granted in? Maryland? Wyoming? What state of the Union?"

"I don't know that either."

Eli surveyed him mournfully. He had taken off his suit coat and the armpits of his white shirt showed a faint bluish tinge.

"It was only mentioned in passing," Ian said. "You don't discuss your divorce in detail with the family of your new husband. So when my brother died, and then Lucy died, there was no one we could ask. She had left behind the three children and we were hoping some of her relatives could take them, but we didn't know if she had any relatives. We didn't even know her maiden name."

Beyond the plate glass window, Sunday traffic swished along Lake Avenue. Sister Bertha said Netta had escaped unburned and so had her husband and baby and her dear, darling, wonderful, incredible little dog.

"Still," Eli said, "your sister-in-law must have had some kind of document. Some certificate or something, somewhere among her papers."

"She didn't leave any papers. After she died my dad went through her house and he couldn't find a one."

"How about her billfold? Driver's license?"

"She didn't drive."

"Social security card?"

"For Lucy Dean. Period."

"Photos, then. Any photos?"

"None."

"Your family must have photos, though. From after she married your brother."

"We do, but my mother put them away so as not to remind the children."

"Not to remind them? Well, land sakes."

"My mother's kind of . . . she prefers to look on the bright side. But I can find them for you, I'm sure."

"Maybe later on," Eli said. "Okay: let's talk about your sister-in-law's friends. You recall if she had any girlfriends?"

"Not close ones," Ian said. "Just a couple of women she waitressed with, back before she married Danny. One of them we never tracked down, and the other my mother ran into a year or so after Lucy died but she said she really didn't know a thing about her."

"Didn't no one ever *ask* this Lucy anything?"

"It does sound peculiar," Ian said. This was the first time he'd realized exactly how peculiar. He was amazed that they could have been so unaware, so incurious, living all those months alongside another human being.

Eli said, "Tell what was in her desk."

"She didn't have a desk."

"Her topmost bureau drawer, then. Or that ragtag drawer full of string and such in her kitchen."

"All I know is, my dad went through her house and he didn't find anything useful. He talked about how people don't write letters anymore."

"So: no letters."

"And no address book, either. I remember he mentioned that."

"How about her divorce papers? She couldn't have throwed them away."

"Maybe after she remarried she did."

"Well, then, her marriage certificate. Her marriage to your brother."

"Nope."

"You know she would've kept that."

"All I can say is, we didn't find it."

"She must've had a safe deposit box."

"Lucy? I doubt it. And where was the key, then?"

"So you are trying to tell me," Eli said, "that a person manages to get through life without a single solitary piece of paper in her possession."

"Well, I realize it's unusual—"

"It's impossible!"

"Well . . ."

"Had her place been burglarized recently? Did the drawers look like they'd been rifled?"

"Not that I heard of," Ian said.

"Was anybody else living in the house with her?"

"No . . ."

But a dim uneasiness flitted past him, like something you see and yet don't see out of the corner of your eye.

"Anyone suspicious hanging about her?"

"No, no . . ."

But wary, suspicious Agatha pushed into his mind—her closed-off face with the puffy lids that veiled her secret thoughts.

"Now, I don't want you to take this wrong," Eli said, "but you are about the most *unhelpful* client I ever had to deal with."

"I realize that. I'm sorry," Ian said. "I shouldn't have wasted your time."

Eli shook his head, and his cowlick waggled and dipped. God's arrow with no place to go, Ian couldn't help thinking.

. . .

Monday noon, he told Mr. Brant he was eating at home today. He drove home and let himself into the house, announcing, "It's me! Forgot my billfold!"

"Oh, hello, dear," his mother called from the kitchen. Then she and his father went on talking, no doubt over their usual lunch of tinned soup and saltine crackers.

He climbed to the second floor and onward, more stealthily, to the attic, to Daphne and Agatha's little room underneath the eaves.

Girls tended to be messier than boys, he thought. (He had noticed that in his college days.) Agatha's bed was heaped with so many books that he wondered how she slept, and Daphne's was a jungle of stuffed animals. He went over to Agatha's bureau, a darkly varnished highboy that had to stand away from the wall a bit so as not to hit the eaves. The top was littered with pencil stubs and used Kleenexes and more books, but the drawers were fairly well organized. He patted each one's contents lightly, alert for something that didn't belong—the rustle of paper or a hard-edged address book. But there was nothing.

He knelt and looked under her bed. Dust balls. He lifted the mattress. Candy-bar wrappers. He shook his head and let the mattress drop. He tried the old fiberboard wardrobe standing at one end of the room and found a rod of clothes, half Daphne's and half Agatha's, packed too tightly together. Shoes and more shoes lay tangled underneath.

He bent to poke his head inside the storage room that ran under the eaves. In the dimness he made out a dress form, a lampshade, two foot lockers, and a cardboard carton. He crawled further inside and lifted one of the carton's flaps. The musty gray smell reminded him of mice. He dragged the carton toward the door for a closer look: his mother's framed college diploma, a bundle of letters addressed to Miss Beatrice Craig . . . He pushed the carton toward the rear again.

Turning to go, he saw a faded, fabric-covered box on the floor—the kind that stationery sometimes comes in. He flipped up the lid and found a clutter of barrettes and hair ribbons and junk jewelry. Agatha's, no doubt. He let the lid fall shut and crawled on out.

In the bedroom, he paused. He reached back and pulled open the drawer in the box's base.

Right away, he knew he'd hit on something. The contents were so tidy: flattened papers stacked in order of size, and on top of them a few pieces of jewelry, no less junky than those in the main compartment but obviously dating from an earlier time. He pushed the jewelry aside and removed the papers.

A savings booklet from Mercantile Safe Deposit and Trust, showing a balance of $123.08. The title to a Chevrolet owned by Daniel C. Bedloe. A receipt from Morehead TV Repair guaranteeing all replacement parts for thirty days. A marriage certificate for Daniel Craig Bedloe and Lucy Ann Dean. (Ian paused a moment over that one. Was there any remote possibility that Ann could be a last name?) A birth certificate for Daphne Marie Bedloe. A pamphlet of instructions for filing health insurance claims. A birth certificate for Agatha Lynn Dulsimore and then one for Thomas. A receipt for—

Agatha *who?*

Agatha Lynn Dulsimore, born April 4, 1959. Father's full name: Thomas Robert Dulsimore. Mother's maiden name: Lucy Ann Dean. And Thomas Robert Dulsimore, Junior; same parents.

Why, Dean was not Lucy's married name but her maiden name. She must have changed back to Dean after the divorce, and changed her children's names too—at least by implication. All this time, the Bedloes had been hunting a man who didn't exist.

Ian sifted through the few remaining papers—a hazy, unflattering photo of Lucy and the older two children, an auto insurance policy, a recipe for banana bread—but the birth certificates were the only items that told him anything. Both listed the parents' home address as Portia, Maryland. Both carried definite dates, and a doctor's name, and a hospital's name in a town called Marcy, which if Ian recollected right lay not far from Portia, just below the Pennsylvania line. He had enough to track a man down by, provided a person was halfway skilled at tracking.

He slipped the papers inside his shirt and went off to see Eli Everjohn.

"Have some mashed potato, Honeybunch," Daphne said. She held her spoon out to the little cat, who was sitting on Daphne's lap with her front paws folded primly beneath her. First the cat peered into Daphne's eyes, as if checking to make sure she really meant it, and then she leaned forward and lapped daintily. When she was finished, the spoon gleamed. She sat up to wash her face. "Good girl," Daphne said, and she dipped the spoon back in her plate and took a mouthful for herself.

"Ooh, revolting!" Agatha said. "Ian, did you see what she did?"

"What? What'd I do?" Daphne asked.

"You ate from a spoon the cat licked!"

At the other end of the table, Thomas gave an elderly cough. "Well, actually," he said, "the cat's the one who should worry. Mr. Pratt says human spit carries more germs than any other animal's, because humans have these fingers they keep putting in their mouths."

Ian laughed. The others looked at him.

"I was just, ah, thinking," he told them.

They looked away again.

You could never call it a penance, to have to take care of these three. They were all that gave his life color, and energy, and . . . well, life.

What he would do was, once he got Eli's report he would file it in a drawer someplace. Then when they grew up and started wondering about their origins he would hand it over to them; that was all. He would certainly not use the information himself in any way.

People needed to know their genetic backgrounds—what diseases ran in their families and so forth. Also this would help him apply for guardianship. Social Security. That sort of thing.

He rose and started clearing the table. It was a relief to have all that settled. He was glad he hadn't told anyone what he was doing.

But at work the next day, he did tell someone. He told Jeannie. He was teaching her how to select the right grain of wood and she asked if he'd like to go to a movie that night at the Charles. "I can't," he said.

"What, are movies against your religion?"

"No, it's my turn to car-pool for Brownies."

"Hey," she said. "Ian. How long you going to go on living like this, anyway?"

So he told her about Eli. He didn't know why, exactly. It wasn't as if finding Thomas Dulsimore would change his situation. Maybe he just hoped to prove he wasn't as passive as she supposed. And she did seem gratifyingly interested. When he mentioned the stationery box she said, "Naw! Go on!" She asked, "What-all was in it?" and she even wanted to know about the jewelry.

"It wasn't the kind of jewelry that would give you any clues," he said. "I honestly didn't pay much attention."

"And the photo?"

"Oh, well, that was . . . well, the detective was glad to see it, of course, so's he'd know more or less what she looked like, but it didn't show a street sign or a license plate or anything like that. Just Lucy."

"Was she pretty?"

"Sure, I guess so."

For some reason, he didn't want to tell her *how* pretty.

Lucy's image swam into his mind—not the real-life version

but the version in the snapshot: out of focus, too young, still unformed, nowhere near as finely chiseled as she had seemed later. One hip was slung out gracelessly to support Thomas's weight, and one hand was reaching blurrily to gather Agatha closer. Against all logic (he knew he was being ridiculous), he started resenting Agatha's disloyalty in keeping her mother's likeness. There you are: you give up school, you sacrifice everything for these children, and what do they do? They secretly hoard their mother's photo and cling to her and prefer her. She hadn't even taken proper care of them, willfully dying and leaving them as she did; but evidently blood motherhood won over everything.

Jeannie said, "I'm really glad to hear you're doing this, Ian."

"Well, it's only so we can get straight," he told her. "I certainly don't plan to hand the three of them over to strangers or anything like that."

"What are you, crazy?" she asked. "You've got a life to live! You can't drag them around with you forever."

"But I'm responsible for them. I worry I'd be, um, sinning, so to speak, to walk away from them."

"You want to know what I think?" Jeannie asked. She leaned forward. Her face seemed sharper now, more pointed. The hollow between her collarbones could have held a teaspoon of salt. "I think you're sinning *not* to walk away," she said.

"How do you figure that?"

"I think we're each allowed one single life to live on this planet. We'll never get another chance in all eternity," she said. "And if you let it go to waste—now, *that* is sinning."

"Yes," he said, "but what if I'm honor-bound to waste it? What if I have an obligation?"

He worried she would make him explain, but she was too caught up in proving her point. "Even then!" she said triumphantly. "You put your regrets behind you. You move on past them. You do not commit the sin of squandering your only life."

"Well, it *sounds* good," he said.

It did sound good. He really had no argument to offer against it.

At Prayer Meeting the following night he looked for Eli Everjohn but didn't find him, or the strawberry blonde either. He spotted Sister Bertha's dark red pompadour and he sat down next to her and asked, "Where's your daughter this evening?"

"She went home."

"Home?"

"Her and Eli both, home to Caro Mill. Eli said to give you a message, though. What was it now he said? He said not to think you had slipped his mind and he would be in touch."

"Thanks," Ian told her.

Then Reverend Emmett announced the opening hymn: "Work for the Night Is Coming."

Every time Ian attended Prayer Meeting, he thought of his first visit here. He remembered how he had felt welcomed by the loving voices of the singers; he remembered the sensation of prayers flowing heavenward. Coming here had saved him, he knew. Without the Church of the Second Chance he would have struggled alone forever, sunk in hopelessness.

So when Prayer Meeting seemed long-winded or inconsequential, when the petitions had to do with minor health complaints and personal disputes, he controlled his impatience. Tonight he prayed for Brother Kenneth's colon to grow less irritable, for Sister Myra's husband to appreciate her more fully. He listened to a recitation from Sister Nell that seemed not so much a request for prayers as an autobiography. "I learned to stop blaming myself for everything that went wrong," one of her paragraphs went. "I had all the time been blaming myself. But really, you know, when you think about it, mostly it's other people to blame, the godless and the self-centered, and so I said to this gal on my shift, I said, 'Now listen here, Miss Maggie. You may think I was the one in charge of the . . .' "

Till Reverend Emmett broke in. "Ah, Sister Nell?"

"What?"

"What would you like us to pray for, exactly?"

"Pray for me to have strength," she said, "in the face of fools and sinners."

Ian prayed for Sister Nell to have strength.

The closing hymn was "Softly and Tenderly," and when they sang, "Come home! Come home!" Ian felt he was the one they were calling.

"Go ye now into the world and bear witness to His teachings," Reverend Emmett said, raising his arms. Almost before his "Amen," people were stirring and preparing to leave. Several spoke to Ian as they passed. "Good to see you, Brother Ian." "How're the kids?" "Coming to paint with us Saturday?" They filed out. Ian hung behind.

Often it seemed to him that this room itself was his source of peace. Even the flicker of the fluorescent lights heartened him, and the faint chemical smell left over from when the place had been a dry cleaner's. He found reasons to loiter, first collecting the hymn pamphlets and then stacking them just so on the counter. He paused at the edges of a conversation between Reverend Emmett and Brother Kenneth, who was offering further details about his colon. He rolled down his shirtsleeves and carefully buttoned his cuffs before, at long last, stepping out the door.

Then behind him, Reverend Emmett said, "Brother Ian? Mind if I walk partway with you?"

Ian felt his shoulders loosen. Possibly, this was what he'd been hoping for all along.

They walked north on York Road through a summerlike night, Reverend Emmett swinging his Bible. He was taller than Ian and took longer strides, although he kept trying to slow down. Occasionally he hummed a few notes beneath his breath—"Softly and Tenderly" again. Ian thought of an evening back in his Boy Scout days, when the scoutmaster (a young, athletic man, a former basketball star) had given him a ride home, filling him with a mixture of joy and self-consciousness. He knew Reverend Emmett merely acted as God's steward, and that for someone who was the church's founder and its sole leader he seemed remarkably unimpressed with his own importance. Still, Ian always felt tongue-tied around him. Tonight he considered discussing the weather but decided that was too mundane, and then when the silence stretched on too long he wished he *had* discussed the weather, but if he brought it up now it would seem strained. So he kept quiet, and it was Reverend Emmett who finally spoke.

"Some Prayer Meetings," he said, "are like cleaning out a closet. Clearing away the dribs and drabs. Necessary, but tedious."

And Ian said, as if making a perfectly apt response: "Is there such a thing as the Devil?"

Reverend Emmett glanced over at him.

"I mean," Ian said, "does someone exist whose purpose is to tempt people into evil? To make them feel torn one way and another so they're not sure which way is right anymore?"

"What is it you're tempted to do, Brother Ian?" Reverend Emmett asked.

Ian swallowed. "I'm wasting my life," he said.

"Excuse me?"

He must have mumbled the words. He raised his chin and said, almost shouting, "I'm wasting the only life I have! I have one single life in this universe and I'm not using it!"

"Well, of course you're using it," Reverend Emmett said calmly.

"I am?"

"This *is* your life," Reverend Emmett said.

They faced each other at an intersection. A woman swerved around them.

"Lean into it, Ian," Reverend Emmett said. Not "Brother Ian," but "Ian." It made what he said sound more direct, more oracular. He said, "View your burden as a gift. It's the theme that has been given you to work with. Accept that, and lean into it. This is the only life you'll have."

Then he clapped Ian on the shoulder, and turned away to cross York Road.

Ian resumed walking. For a while he pondered Reverend Emmett's message, but he didn't find it much help. To tell the truth, the man had disappointed him. And besides, he hadn't answered Ian's question. The question was: Is there such a thing as the Devil?

Ian had been referring to Jeannie, of course—Jeannie sitting forward compellingly, the hollow deepening at the base of her throat as she tempted him from his path. But the face that came to his mind at this moment was not Jeannie's. It was Lucy's. It was the tiny, perfect, heart-shaped face of Lucy Dean.

"Honeybunch has worms," Agatha told Ian.

"How do you know that?"

"You really want me to say?"

"On second thought, never mind," Ian said. "So, what? We have to take her to the vet?"

"I made an appointment: tomorrow afternoon at four."

She and Thomas sat on either side of Ian in the porch swing, enjoying the last of a golden autumn day. Down on the front walk, Daphne was playing hopscotch with the Carter girl and the newlyweds' five-year-old. "You did step on the line, Tracy. You did," she said in her raucous little voice.

Ian said, "Maybe Grandpa could drive you. I could leave the car with him tomorrow and take the bus."

"We like it better when *you* come," Agatha said.

"Well, but I have work."

"Please, Ian," Thomas said. "Grandpa drove us when we went to get her cat shots and he yelled at her for sitting on his foot."

"His accelerator foot," Agatha explained.

"We like it better when you're there, acting in charge," Thomas told him.

Ian looked at him a moment. His mind had drifted elsewhere. "Thomas," he said, "remember that big doll you used to carry around?"

"Oh, well, that was a long time ago," Thomas said.

"Yes, but I was wondering. How come you named her Dulcimer?"

"I don't even know where she is anymore. I don't know why I named her that," Thomas said.

He seemed embarrassed, rather than secretive. And Agatha wasn't listening. You'd think she would suspect; she was the one who'd kept that box hidden away. But she stirred the porch swing dreamily with one foot. "Suppose we got bombed," she said to Ian.

"Pardon?"

He saw the stationery box in his mind: the dust on the lid, the congealed sheaf of papers. She must not have glanced inside for years, he realized. She might even have forgotten it existed.

"Suppose Baltimore got atom-bombed," she was saying. "Know what I'd do?"

"You wouldn't do a thing," Thomas told her. "You'd be dead."

"No, seriously. I've been thinking. I'd break into a supermarket, and I'd settle our family inside. That way we'd have all the supplies we needed. Canned goods and bottled goods, enough to last us forever."

"Well, not forever," Thomas said.

"Long enough to get over the radiation, though."

"Not a chance. Right, Ian?"

Ian said, "Hmm?"

"The radiation would last for years, right?"

"Well, so would the canned goods," Agatha said. "And if we still had electricity—"

"Electricity! Ha!" Thomas said. "Do you ever live in a dream world!"

"Well, even without electricity," Agatha said stubbornly, "we could manage. Nowadays supermarkets sell blankets, even. And socks! And prescription drugs, the bigger places. We could get penicillin and stuff. And some way we'd bring Claudia and them from Pittsburgh, I haven't figured just how, yet—"

"Forget it, Ag," Thomas told her. "That's ten more mouths to feed."

"But we *need* a lot of kids. They're the future generation. And Grandma and Grandpa are the old folks who would teach us how to carry on."

"How about Ian?" Thomas asked.

"How about him?"

"He's not old. And he's not the future generation, either. You have to draw the line somewhere."

"Gee, thanks," Ian said, lazily toeing the swing. But Agatha turned a pensive gaze on him.

"No," she said finally, "Ian comes too. He's the one who keeps us all together."

"The cowpoke of the family, so to speak," Ian told Thomas. But he felt touched. And when his father called from the doorway—"Ian? Telephone"—he rested a palm on Agatha's thick black hair a second as he rose.

The receiver lay next to the phone on the front hall table. He picked it up and said, "Hello?"

"Brother Ian? Wallah," a man said from a distance.

"Pardon?"

"This is Eli Everjohn. Wallah, I said."

"Wallah?"

"Wallah! I found your man."

"You . . . what?"

"Except he's dead," Eli said.

Ian leaned one shoulder against the wall.

"Appears he didn't live much past what your sister-in-law did. Hello? Are you there?"

"I'm here."

"Maybe this is a shock."

"No, that's all right," Ian said.

The shock was not Tom Dulsimore's death but the fact that he had lived at all—that someone else in the world had turned up actual evidence of him.

But Eli started breaking the news all over again, this time more delicately. "I'm sorry to have to tell you that Thomas Dulsimore, Senior has passed away," he said. "Had himself a motorcycle crash back in nineteen sixty-seven."

" 'Sixty-seven," Ian said.

"Seems he was one of those folks that don't hold with helmets."

So Tom Dulsimore was not an option anymore—not even in Ian's fantasies.

"Reason I know is, I phoned his mother. Mrs. Millet. She'd remarried, is the reason it took me a while. I told her I was a buddy of Tom's wanting to get in touch with him. I didn't say no more though till I got your say-so. Should I go ahead now and pay her a visit?"

"No, never mind."

"She's bound to know the kids' relatives. Small-town kind of lady; you could just tell she would know all about it."

"Maybe I should get her address," Ian said.

"Okay, suit yourself. Mrs. Margie Millet. Forty-three Orchard Road, Portia, Maryland. You need to write that down?"

"I have it," Ian said. (He would have it forever, he felt—chiseled into his brain.) "Thanks, Eli. I appreciate your help. You know where to send the bill."

"Aw, it won't amount to much. This one was easy."

For you, maybe, Ian thought. He told Eli goodbye and hung up.

From the kitchen, his mother called, "Agatha? Time to set the table!"

"Coming."

Ian met Agatha at the door and stepped past her onto the porch. She didn't notice a thing.

The evening was several shades darker now, as if curtain after curtain had fallen in his absence. Thomas was swinging the swing hard enough to make the chains creak, and down on the sidewalk the little girls were still playing hopscotch. Ian paused to watch them. Something about the purposeful planting of small shoes within chalked squares tugged at him. He leaned on the railing and thought, *What does this remind me of? What? What?* Daphne tossed the pebble she used as a marker and it landed in the farthest square so crisply, so ringingly, that the sound seemed thrown back from a sky no higher than a ceiling, cupping all of Waverly Street just a few feet overhead.

"Lucy Ann Dean was as common as dirt," Mrs. Millet said. "I know I shouldn't speak ill of the dead, but there's just no getting around it: she was common."

They were sitting in Mrs. Millet's Pennsylvania Dutch–style breakfast nook, all blue painted wood and cut-out hearts and tulips. (Her house was the kind where the living room waited in reserve for some momentous occasion that never arrived, and Ian had caught no more than a glimpse of its white shag rugs and white upholstery on his journey to the kitchen.) Mrs. Millet slouched across from him, opening a pack of cigarettes. She was younger than he had expected, with a very stiff, very brown hairdo and a hatchet face. Her magenta minidress struck him as out-dated, although Ian was not the last word on fashion.

He himself wore a suit and tie, chosen with an eye to looking trustworthy. After all, how did she know he wasn't some knock-and-rob man? He hadn't phoned ahead because he hadn't fully acknowledged he was planning this; he had dressed this morning only for church, he told himself, although he almost never wore a tie to church. After services he had eaten Sunday dinner with his family and then (yawning aloud and stretching in a stagy manner) had announced he was feeling so restless, he thought he might go for a drive. Whereupon he had headed north without consulting a map, relying on the proper road signs to appear or else not, as the case might be. And they did appear. The signs for Portia, the signs for Orchard Road. The giant brass 43 glittering, almost shouting, from the lamppost in front of the redwood cottage. "My name is Ian Bedloe," he had said when she opened the door. "I hope I'm not disturbing you, but I'm Lucy Dean's brother-in-law and I'm trying to locate some of her family."

She hadn't exactly slammed the door in his face, but her expression had frozen over somehow. "Then maybe you better ask *her*," she told him.

"Ask who?"

"Why, Lucy Dean, of course."

"But . . . Lucy's dead," he said.

She stared at him.

"She died a long time ago," he told her.

"Well," she said, "I'd be fibbing if I said I was sorry. I always knew she was up to no good."

He was shamed by the rush of pleasure he felt—the bitter, wicked pleasure of hearing someone else agree with him at long last.

Now she said, "First off, her parents drank." She took a cigarette from her pack and tamped it against the table. "How do you suppose they had that car wreck? Three sheets to the wind, both of them. Then her aunt Alice moved in with her, and she was just plain cracked, if you want my honest opinion. I don't think the two of them had anything to do with each other. It's more like Lucy just raised herself. Well, for that much I give her credit: she'd come out of that run-down shack every morning neat as a pin, every hair in place, every accessory matching, which heaven knows how she did on their little pittance of money . . ."

She stole it, is how. Shoplifted. Not even you know the worst of it.

". . . and she'd sashay off to school all prissy and Miss America

with her books held in front of her chest. The boys were fools
for her, but my Tommy was the only one she'd look at. You
should've seen my Tommy. He was movie-star handsome. He
could pass for Tony Curtis, ought to give you some idea. He and
Lucy went steady from ninth grade on. Went to every dance and
sports event together. Well, excepting Junior Prom. They had a
little disagreement the week before Junior Prom and she went
with Gary Durbin, but Tommy beat Gary to a pulp next morning
and him and Lucy got back together. At their Senior Prom
they were King and Queen. I still have the pictures. Tommy
wore a tux and he looked good enough to eat. I said, 'Tommy,
you could have any girl you wanted,' but then, well, you
guessed it."

She lit her cigarette and tilted her head and blew out a long
stream of smoke, all the while staring defiantly at Ian. He said,
"I did?"

"Lucy went and got herself pregnant."

"Oh."

"I said, 'Tommy, you can't be certain that baby's even yours,'
and he said, 'Mom, I know it. I just don't know what on earth
I'm going to do,' he told me."

Ian said, "What?" He felt he'd missed something. "You mean
it could have been someone else's baby?" he asked.

"Well, who can say?" Mrs. Millet said. "I mean life is all so
iffy, right? I said, 'Tommy, *don't* fall for this! You could be
anything! You could be a male model, even! Why saddle yourself
with a wife and kid?' But Lucy talked him into it. She had him
wrapped around her little finger, I tell you. It was the kind of
thing that just breaks a mother's heart."

"So . . . but this aunt of hers," Ian said. He seemed to be
losing track of the purpose of his visit. "Alice, you say."

"Alice Dean. Well, she had nothing against it. She was delighted to marry Lucy off. Meant she could get back to wherever
she came from and her old-maid ways. So Tommy and Lucy set
up house in this crummy little trailer over at Blalock's Trailer

Park and Tommy started work at Luther's Sports Equipment, but when Lucy told him she was expecting *again*—two babies in three years!—he left her. I don't blame him, either. I do not blame him. He was just a boy! 'When you going to do this, when you going to do that?' she was always asking, but he hadn't had him any kind of life yet! *Naturally* he wanted to roam a bit. She claimed he was irresponsible and she fretted about the least little thing, so of course he stayed away even more and when he did come home they'd fight. Twice the police had to be called. Then thank the Lord, he finally had the sense to leave. Got shed of her and asked for a divorce. And wouldn't you know she hired herself a big-shot city lawyer and sued for child support. Proves what I'd been telling him: all as she was after was his money. Someone to support those kids; by then she'd had the second one and she was always yammering about, 'I can't feed these kids on yard weeds,' and such. I told Tommy, I said, 'She should just go to work, if she needs money so bad.' "

"But then who would watch the children?" Ian asked.

"Lord, you sound just like her. 'Then who would watch the children?' " Mrs. Millet mimicked in a high voice. She flicked her cigarette into a tin ashtray. "She should've got a sitter, of course. That's what I told Tommy. 'And don't expect *me* to sit,' I told him. I never did like other people's children much. So anyhow, Tommy hung around here a whiles but there wasn't all that much for him in Portia, and so finally he hitchhiked to Wyoming. He had in mind to find work there, something glamorous having to do with horses. Well, that didn't quite come through like he had hoped and so of course he couldn't send money first thing, but he was planning to! And then we hear Lucy's run off."

"Run off?"

"Run away with some man. That lawyer that handled her divorce. It was Mr. Blalock called and told me, down at the trailer park. She owed him rent. He said her trailer was empty as last year's bird nest, door flapping open in the wind and everything hauled away that wasn't nailed down. Said her neighbors saw a moving van come to take her belongings. Not a U-Haul; a professional van. The man was loaded, was what they guessed. She must've went with him for the money."

"Went with him where?" Ian asked.

"Why, to Baltimore, but at first we didn't know that. At first we had no idea, and I told Tommy he was better off that way. 'The slate has been wiped clean,' I told him on the phone. 'I do believe we've seen the last of her.' But *then* guess what. She calls him up a few months later. Calls him in Cheyenne. Tells him she's in Baltimore and wants the money he owes her. Oh, I just wish I'd have been on the other end of the line. I'd have hung up on her so fast! But Tommy, I will say, he was a whole lot smarter by then. He says, 'I thought you had yourself some rich guy now,' and she says, 'Oh,' says, 'that didn't work out.' Well, I just bet it didn't work out. I bet the fellow was married, was what. That's the kind of thing you see happen every day. Tommy tells her, 'I can't help *that*, I met somebody here and we're planning on a June wedding. All I got is going for the wedding,' he says. Then he says, 'And anyhow, where's my things? You took every blasted thing I left in that trailer,' he says. 'Stuff I was coming back to fetch someday you packed up and hauled away like it belonged to you.' 'Tommy, I need money,' she says. 'I'm in a awful fix right now.' He says, 'First you send me my things,' and signs off. You see how he'd got wise to her. Oh, she aged him, I tell you. She hardened him. She callused him."

Mrs. Millet stubbed out her cigarette and sat staring into space. Over the stove, a plastic clock in the shape of a cat ticked its long striped tail back and forth.

"It was the winter of 'sixty-seven he had the accident," she said. "Motorcycling on icy roads. His wife called me up and told me. I will never hear the phone ring again as long as I live without going all over cold and sick."

Ian said, "Well, I'm sorry."

But it was only the most detached and courteous kind of

sorry. He would never have left the children with such a man, even if the man had been willing.

"Of course, that second wife was pretty no-account herself," Mrs. Millet said.

Ian stood up. (No use staying on for more of this.) He said, "Mrs. Millet, I appreciate your talking to me. I guess what you're saying is, there was only that one aunt."

"That's all as *I* ever heard of," she said.

"And no brothers or sisters, or cousins, or anything like that."

"Not as I know of. Chances are the aunt has passed on too, by this time. Lord, lately it seems the whole world has passed on."

It did seem that way, at times. At times, it really did.

At Prayer Meeting the ghostly smell of dry-cleaning fluid mingled with Mrs. Jordan's cologne. "Pray for me to accept this cross without complaint," Sister Myra said. Accept what cross? Ian hadn't been listening. He bowed his head and felt the silence wrap around him like a clean, cool sheet that you reach for in your sleep halfway through a hot night.

"For our Sister Myra," Reverend Emmett said at last.

"Amen."

"Any other prayers, any other prayers . . ."

In a row toward the rear, Sister Bertha stood up. "I am troubled in my heart for another person tonight," she said. She spoke pointedly to the empty chair in front of her. "I know of someone here who seems to be experiencing a serious difficulty. I was waiting to see if he'd ask for our prayers but so far he hasn't."

He? There were only three men present: Reverend Emmett, Brother Kenneth, and Ian.

"I know," Sister Bertha said, "that this person must be feeling very overworked, very beset with problems, and he's casting about for a solution. But it doesn't seem to occur to him that he could bring it up at Prayer Meeting."

She sat down.

Ian's cheeks felt hot.

Surely private detectives were sworn to secrecy, weren't they? Just like lawyers, or doctors. Weren't they?

Reverend Emmett looked uncertain. He said, "Well . . ." and glanced around at the other worshipers. His eyes did not linger noticeably on Ian, although of course he must suspect. "Does this person wish to ask for our prayers?" he said.

No response. Just a few rustles and whispers.

"In that case," Reverend Emmett said, "we won't intrude. Let us pray, instead, for *all* of us. For all of us to know that we can bring our problems to God whenever we feel ready to let go of them."

He raised his arms and the silence fell, as if he had somehow cast it forth in front of him.

Sister Bertha is a nosy-bones, Ian thought distinctly. *And I hate that tomato-soup color she dyes her hair.*

After the Benediction, he was the first one out the door. He left behind even Mrs. Jordan, who most likely would want to walk home with him, and he set off at a brisk, angry pace. So the last thing he expected to hear was Reverend Emmett calling his name. "Brother Ian!"

Ian stopped and turned.

The man must have run the whole way. He must have left his flock unattended, his Bible open on the counter, his church lit up and unlocked. But he wasn't even breathing hard. He approached at a saunter, seemingly absorbed in slipping on a cardigan the same color as the dusk.

"May I tag along?" he asked.

Ian shrugged.

They set off together more slowly.

"Of course, it does come down to whether a person feels ready to let go," Reverend Emmett said in the most conversational tone.

Ian kicked a Dixie cup out of his path.

"Some people prefer to hug their problems to themselves," Reverend Emmett said.

Ian wheeled on him, clenching his fists in his pockets. He said, *"This* is my life? This is all I get? It's so settled! It's so cut and dried! After this there's no changing! I just lean into the burden of those children forever, is that what you're saying?"

"No," Reverend Emmett told him.

"You said that! You said to lean into my burden!"

"But those children will be grown in no time," Reverend Emmett said. *"They* are not the burden I meant. The burden is forgiveness."

"Okay," Ian said. "Fine. How much longer till I'm forgiven?"

"No, no. The burden is that *you* must forgive."

"Me?" Ian said. He stared at Reverend Emmett. "Forgive who?"

"Why, your brother and his wife, of course."

Ian said nothing.

Finally Reverend Emmett asked, "Shall we walk on?"

So they did. They passed a lone man waiting at a bus stop, a shopkeeper locking up his store. Each footstep, Ian felt, led him closer to something important. He was acutely conscious all at once of motion, of flux and possibility. He felt he was an arrow—not an arrow shot by God but an arrow heading toward God, and if it took every bit of this only life he had, he believed that he would get there in the end.

7

Organized Marriage

It was Agatha who came up with the notion of finding Ian a wife. Agatha was graduating that June; she'd had word she'd been accepted at her first-choice college; she would soon be leaving the family forever. And one night in April she walked into the living room and told the other two, "I'm worried about Ian."

Thomas and Daphne glanced over at her. (There was a commercial on just then, anyhow.) She stood in the doorway with her arms folded, her tortoiseshell glasses propped on top of her head in a purposeful, no-nonsense manner. "Who will keep him company after we're gone?" she asked.

"You're the only one going," Daphne told her. "He's still got me and Thomas."

"Not for long," Agatha said.

10

Recovering from the Hearts-of-Palm Flu

She asked if he thought he might ever want children and he said, "Oh, well, maybe sometime." She asked how long he figured they should wait and he said, "A few years, maybe? I don't know."

They'd been married just four months, by then. He could see his answer came as a disappointment.

But why should they rush to change things? Their lives were perfect. Simply watching her—simply sitting at the kitchen table watching her knead a loaf of bread—filled him with contentment. Her hands were so capable, and she moved with such economy. When she wiped her floury palms on the seat of her jeans, he was struck with admiration for her naturalness.

"I had been wondering about sooner," she told him.

"Well, no need to decide this instant," he said.

He watched her oil a baking pan, working her long, tanned fingers deftly into the corners, and he thought of a teacher he had had in seventh grade. Mrs. Arnett, her name was. Mrs. Arnett had once been his ideal woman—soft curves and sweet perfume and ivory skin. He had found any number of reasons to bicycle past her house. Her front bow window, which was curtained off day and night by cream-colored draperies, had displayed a single, pale blue urn, and somehow that urn had come to represent all his fantasies about marriage. He had imagined Mrs. Arnett greeting her husband at the door each evening, wearing not the bermudas or dull slacks his mother wore but a swirly dress the same shade of blue as the urn; and she would kiss Mr. Arnett full on the lips and lead him inside. Everything would be so focused. No distractions: no TV blaring or telephone ringing or neighbors stopping by.

Certainly no children.

You couldn't say Ian and Rita lived that way, even now. They were still in the house on Waverly Street—partly a matter of economics, partly to keep his father company. (Daphne had a place of her own now.) His father still occupied the master bedroom, and Rita's widowed mother was forever dropping by, and Rita's various aunts and cousins and a whole battalion of woman friends sat permanently around the kitchen table waiting for her to pour coffee. Where would children fit into all this?

"Next birthday, I'll be thirty," Rita told him.

"Thirty's young," Ian said.

Next birthday, Ian would be forty-two.

Forty-two seemed way too old to be thinking of babies.

At the wood shop, one of the workers had a daughter smaller than his own granddaughters. He was on his second wife, a manicurist named LaRue, and LaRue had told him it wasn't fair to deprive her of a family just because he had already had the joy of one. He had reported every detail of their arguments on the subject; and next he'd discussed the pregnancy, which seemed so new and exciting to LaRue and so old to Butch, and finally the baby herself, who cried every evening and interrupted dinner and caused LaRue to smell continually of spit-up milk. Now the baby was two and sometimes came along with her mother to give Butch a ride home after work. She would toddle through the shavings, crowing, and hold out her little arms until he set aside his plane and picked her up. "Ain't she a doll?" he asked the others. "Ain't she a living doll?" But the sight of his grizzled cheek next to that flower-petal face was disturbing, somehow, and Ian always turned away, smiling falsely, and grew very busy with his tools.

Ian and Rita went to church on foot that next Sunday because the weather was so fine. Besides, Ian liked the ceremony of it: the two of them holding hands as they walked and calling out greetings to various neighbors working in their yards. Rita wore a dress (or at least, a long black T-shirt that hit her above the knees), because she'd grown up at Alameda Baptist and considered jeans unsuitable for church. Her braid was wound in a knot at the nape of her neck. Ian couldn't help noticing the unusually attractive way her hair grew, hugging her temples closely and swooping down over her ears in ripples.

"Did I tell you Mary-Clay went in for her ultrasound?" she asked. "Her doctor said she's having twins."

"Twins! Good grief," he said. A shadow fell over him.

"Two little girls, her doctor thinks. Mary-Clay is just tickled to bits. Girls are easier than boys, she says."

"Rita," Ian said, "neither is easy."

She glanced at him. He hadn't meant to sound so emphatic.

"At least," he said, "not according to my limited experience."

They turned onto York Road. Ahead they could see a cluster of worshipers standing in front of the church, enjoying their last few moments of sunshine before they stepped inside. Rita said,

"Well, now that you mention it, your experience *was* limited. Those children weren't your own. You weren't even solely responsible for them!"

"Right," Ian told her. "I had both my parents helping, and still it wasn't easy. A lot of it was just plain boring. Just providing a warm body, just *being* there; anyone could have done it. And then other parts were terrifying. Kids get into so much! They start to matter so much. Some days I felt like a fireman or a lifeguard or something—all that tedium, broken up by little spurts of high drama."

Rita gathered a breath, but by then they'd reached the others. Sister Myra said, "Why, hello, you two!" and kissed them both, even Ian. She had never kissed Ian before he was married. Marriage changed things a good deal, he had learned.

They were the church's only newlyweds at the moment, and almost the only ones ever. Their wedding had taken place at Alameda Baptist, but most of Second Chance had attended and Reverend Emmett had helped officiate, even donning one of Alameda's flowing black pastoral robes so when he raised his arms to pray he had resembled a skinny Stealth bomber. Now they were passed from hand to hand like babies in an old folks' home, with Rita saying those just-right things that women somehow know to say. "Brother Kenneth, how's that sciatica? Why, Sister Denise! You've gone and lightened your hair." Ian was impressed, but also disconcerted. This never seemed to be *his* Rita, who spent her weekdays bluntly informing customers that most of their lifelong treasures belonged in the nearest landfill.

They went inside and took two seats halfway up the aisle. Sister Nell was passing out hymn pamphlets. When Ian opened his he found the top corner of each page torn off as if gnawed by a mouse, and he smiled to himself and looked around for Daphne. (She must have some kind of deficiency, Agatha always said, to eat paper the way she did.) But he didn't see her. The fact was that she attended less and less, now that she lived downtown. Just about all you could count on her for was Good Works on Saturday mornings.

Rita was talking with her neighbor on the other side, Brother Kenneth's son Johnny, who used to be a little pipsqueak of a boy but now was studying for the ministry. Sometimes lately he had assisted with the services. Today, though, Reverend Emmett rose alone to deliver the opening prayer. Rita faced forward obediently and bowed her head, but Ian sensed she wasn't listening. She failed to straighten when Reverend Emmett said, "Amen," and she chewed a thumbnail edgily during the Bible reading. Ian reached over and captured her hand and tucked it into his, and she relaxed against him.

"Thus concludes the reading of the Holy Word," Reverend Emmett said. "We will now sing hymn fourteen."

The little organ wheezed out the first notes and Ian let go of Rita's hand. But she didn't draw away. Instead she looked directly into his face as they stood up, ignoring the hymnal he held before them.

"Listen," she said in a low voice. "I think I might be pregnant."

He had already opened his mouth to start singing. He shut it. The congregation went on without them: "Break Thou the bread of life . . ."

"It wasn't on purpose," she said. And then she whispered, "But I intend to be glad about this, I tell you!"

What could he say?

"Me, too, sweetheart," he said.

They faced front again. Stammering slightly, he found his place and joined the other singers.

That was in July. By September, she was having to leave the waistband of her jeans unsnapped and she wore her loosest work shirts over them. She said she thought she could feel the baby moving now—a little bubble, she said, flitting here and there in a larking sort of way. Ian set a palm on her abdomen but it was still too early for him to feel anything from outside.

She bought a book that showed what the baby looked like

week by week, and she and Ian studied it together. A lima bean. A tadpole. Then finally a person but a clumsily constructed one, like something modeled in preschool. They were thinking of Joshua for a boy and Rachel for a girl. Ian tried the names on his tongue to see how they'd work in everyday life. "Oh, and I'd like you to meet my son, Joshua Bedloe . . ." His son! The notion brought forth the most bewildering mixture of feelings: worry and excitement and also, underneath, a pervasive sense of tiredness. He told Rita about everything but the tiredness. That he kept to himself.

Now it seemed the household was completely taken over by women. Rita's batty mother, Bobbeen, spent hours in their kitchen, generally seated not at the table but on it and dangling her high-heeled sandals from her toes. With her crackling, bleached-out fan of hair and snapping gum and staticky barrage of advice, she seemed electric, almost dangerous. "You're insane to go on working when you don't have to, Rita, stark staring insane. Don't you remember what happened to your aunt Dora when *she* kept on? You tell her, Ian. Tell her to quit hauling other folkses' junk when she's four and a half months gone and all her pelvic bones are coming off their hinges." But she didn't actually mean for Ian to say anything; she didn't leave the briefest pause before starting a new train of thought. "I guess you heard about Molly Sidney. Six months along and she phones her doctor, says, 'Feels like somebody's hauling rope out of way down low in my back.' 'Oh,' her doctor says, 'That's normal.' Says, 'Pay it no mind,' and the very next night guess what."

She could recite the most bizarre stories: umbilical cords kinked off like twisted vacuum-cleaner hoses, babies arriving with tails and coats of fur, deluges of blood in the lawn-care aisle at Ace Hardware. If Rita's two married girlfriends were around they would tut-tut. "Hush, now! You'll scare her!" they'd say. But their own stories were nearly as alarming. "I was in labor for thirty-three hours." "Well, they had to tie *me* down on the bed." Serenely, Rita circulated with the coffeepot. Ian retreated to the basement, where his father was repainting the family high chair. "Women!" Ian said. "They're giving me the chills."

"You want to close that door behind you, Ian," his father said. "It was paint fumes caused your cousin Linley's baby to have that little learning problem."

In October Ian started building a cradle of Virginia cherry—a simple slant-sided box without a hood because Rita wanted the baby to be able to see the world. He obtained the materials at no cost but of course he had to contribute his own time, and so he fell into the habit of staying on in the shop after it closed. His metal rasp, zipping down the edge of a rocker slat, said *careen! careen!* Often he seemed to hear the other workers' voices echoing through the empty room. "Drove a spindle wedge too hard and split the goddamn . . ." Bert said clearly, and Mr. Brant asked, "Why the hell you choose a plank with the sapwood showing?" Ian stopped rasping and ran a hand along the slat's edge, trying to gauge the curve. All his years here, he had worked with straight lines. He had deliberately stayed away from the bow-backed chairs and benches that required eye judgment, personal opinion. Now he was surprised at how these two shallow U shapes satisfied his palm.

And all his years here he had failed to understand Mr. Brant's prejudice against nails, his insistence on mortise-and-tenon and dovetails. "You put a drawer together with dovetail, it stays tight a century no matter what the weather," Mr. Brant was fond of saying, and Ian always thought, *A century! Who cares?* It was not that he opposed doing a thing well. Everything that came from his hands was fine and smooth and sturdy. But you could manage that with nails too, for heaven's sake; and if it didn't last forever, why, *he* would not be there to notice. Now, though, he took special pride in the cradle's nearly seamless joints, which would expand and contract in harmony and continue to stay tight through a hundred steamy summers and parched winters.

. . .

Early in December Rita and Ian went with Daphne and her new boyfriend, Curt, to a bar downtown that featured pinball machines. Daphne had developed a passion for pinball. Rita was beginning her seventh month and she had lately cut her work hours in half, which left her with too much time on her hands. Any outing at all struck her as preferable to staying home. This was why Ian agreed to go to the bar, even though he didn't drink. And Rita, of course, couldn't drink, and Curt turned out to belong to A.A. So there the three of them sat with their seltzers while Daphne, merrily sloshing her beer, toured the various games. Her favorite, she said, was the one called Black Knight 2000, which she wanted the four of them to try if only the others would give them half a chance. She hoisted herself onto a stool and glowered at the crowd. There were so many people here that Ian couldn't even see what kind of room it was.

Curt was telling Rita about his sister's breech baby. (Did people actively *collect* these tales?) He didn't look like much, in Ian's honest opinion—a bespectacled and bearded type in clothes too determinedly rustic. Also, something unfortunate had happened to his hair. It stuck out all over his head in rigid little cylinders. Ian said, "What . . . ?" He leaned closer to Daphne and said, "What would you call that kind of hairdo, exactly?"

"Do you like it? I did it myself," she said. "You braid dozens and dozens of eentsy braids and dunk them in Elmer's glue to make them last. The only problem is when he jogs."

"Jogs?"

"He claims they bobble against his head and bang his scalp."

Ian snorted, but all at once he felt old. In fact he was very likely the oldest person present. He looked down at the hand encircling his glass—the grainy skin on his knuckles, the gnarled veins in his forearm. How could he have assumed that old people were born that way? That age was an individual trait, like freckles or blond hair, that would never happen to him?

He was older now, he thought with a thud, than Danny had ever managed to become.

Rita was laughing at something Curt had said, unconsciously cradling the bulge of her baby as she leaned back against the bar. Daphne was humming along with the jukebox. "Madonna," she broke off to tell Ian.

"Pardon?"

" 'Like a Prayer.' "

"I beg your pardon?"

"The *song*, Ian."

"Oh."

He took a gulp from his glass. (This seltzer smelled like wet dog.) "So anyhow," he said to Daphne, "where did you and Curt meet?"

"At work," she said.

Daphne had a job now at a place called Trips Unlimited. Ian said, "He's a travel agent?"

"No, no, he came in to reserve a flight. By profession he's an inventor."

"An inventor."

"He's got this one invention: a Leaf Paw. This sort of claw-type contraption you hold in your left hand to scoop up the leaves you're raking. We think it's going to make him rich."

Ian glanced over at Rita, hoping she'd heard. (They often considered the same things funny.) But Rita was staring fixedly across the room. He followed her eyes and saw a small, pretty girl in a Danzig T-shirt playing the Black Knight 2000 machine. An old friend, maybe? But when he turned back to ask, he realized Rita's stare was unfocused. It was the glazed and inward stare of someone listening to faraway music. He said, "Rita?"

"Excuse me," she said abruptly. She stood and made her way through the crowd, disappearing behind the door marked LADIES.

Ian and Daphne looked at each other. "Think I should go after her?" Daphne asked.

"I'm not sure," he said. "Well, she's probably okay."

Although he was nowhere near as confident as he sounded.

They fell silent. Even Curt seemed to know better than to try and make small talk. Now Ian noticed the noise in this place— the laughter and clinking glassware and the hubbub from the pinball machines, which whanged and burbled and barked instructions in metallic, hollow voices. Everyone was so carefree! Two stools over, a young woman with long hair as dark as Rita's nonchalantly swung her pink-and-turquoise mountain-climbing shoes. A young man in a red jacket and a straight blond ponytail passed her one of the beers he'd just paid for. The jukebox had stopped playing, but some people in a booth were singing "Happy Birthday."

Then Rita was back, white-faced. All three of them stood up. She told Ian, "I'm bleeding."

He swallowed.

Curt was the first to react. He said, "I'll get the check. You three head out to the car," and he dropped a set of keys into Ian's palm.

Ian had forgotten that they'd driven here in Curt's Volvo. "Let's go," he said. He shepherded Rita toward the door. Daphne followed with their wraps. When they reached the sidewalk he stopped to help Rita into her jacket. She shook her head, but he could hear how her teeth were chattering. "Put it on," he told her, and she submitted, allowing him to bully her arms into the sleeves.

Curt caught up with them as Ian was unlocking the car door. "Which hospital?" he asked, sliding behind the wheel, and he started the engine in one smooth motion. He drove as if he'd dealt with such crises often, swooping dexterously from lane to lane and barely slowing for red lights before proceeding through them. Meanwhile Ian held both of Rita's hands in his. Her teeth were still chattering and he wondered if she was in shock.

At the Emergency Room entrance, Curt pulled up behind an ambulance. Ian hustled Rita out of the backseat and took her inside to a woman at a long green counter. "She's bleeding," he told the woman.

"How much?" she asked.

Instantly, he felt reassured. It appeared there were degrees to this; they shouldn't automatically assume the worst. Rita said, "Not a whole lot."

The woman called for a nurse, and Rita was led away while Ian stayed behind to fill out forms. Insurance company, date of birth . . . He answered hurriedly, scrawling across the dotted lines. When he was almost finished, Daphne and Curt came in from parking the car. "They've taken her somewhere," he told them. He asked Daphne, "Do you know her mother's maiden name?"

"Make one up," Daphne said. She looked around at the faded green walls, the elderly black man half asleep on a molded plastic chair. "Not bad," she said. "Usually this place is packed."

How often did she come here, anyway? And Curt, standing behind her, said, "Lord, yes, there've been times I've waited six and seven hours."

"Well, we might have a wait this evening, too," Ian said. "Maybe you should both go home."

"I'm staying," Daphne told him.

"Yes, but," Ian said. He slid the form across the counter to the woman. He said, "But, um, I'd really *rather* you go. To tell the truth."

He could see she felt hurt. She said, "Oh."

"I just want to . . . concentrate on this. All right?" he asked.

"I could concentrate too," she said.

But Curt touched her sleeve and said, "Come on, Daph. I'm sure he'll call as soon as he has anything to tell you."

When he led her away, Ian felt overwhelmingly grateful. He felt he might even love the boy.

Rita lay on a stretcher in an enclosure formed by white curtains. No one had come to examine her yet, she said, but they'd phoned her doctor. She wore a withered blue hospital gown, and a white sheet covered her legs and rose gently over the mound of her stomach. Ian settled on a stool beside the stretcher. He picked up her hand, which felt warmer now and slightly moist. She curled her fingers tightly around his.

"Remember our wedding night?" she asked him.

"Yes, of course."

"Remember in the hotel? I came out of the bathroom in my nightgown and you were sitting on the edge of the bed, touching two fingers to your forehead. I thought you were nervous about making love."

"Well, I was," he said.

"You were praying."

"Well, that too."

"You were shy about saying your bedtime prayers in front of me and so you pretended you were just sort of thinking."

"I was worried I would look like one of those show-off Christians," he said. "But still I wanted to, um, I felt I ought to—"

"Could you pray now?" she asked him.

"Now?"

"Could you pray for the baby?"

"Honey, I've been praying ever since we left the bar," he said.

Really his prayers had been for Rita. He had fixed her firmly, fiercely to this planet and held her there with all his strength. But he had prayed not only for her health but for her happiness, and so in a sense he supposed you could say that he'd prayed for the baby as well.

She spent one night in the hospital but was released the following morning, still pregnant, with orders to lie flat until her due date. At first this seemed easy. She would do anything, she said, anything at all. She would stand on her head for two months, if it helped her hang onto this baby. But she had always been the athletic, go-getter type, and books didn't interest her and TV made her restless. So every evening when Ian came home from work he found the radio blaring, and Rita on the telephone, and the kitchen bustling with women fixing tidbits to tempt her appetite as if she were a delicate invalid. Which, of course, she wasn't. "I don't care if it takes major surgery!" she'd be shouting into the phone. "You get those moldy old magazines *away* from her!" (She was talking to Dennis or Lionel—one of her poor frazzled assistants.) Her hair flared rebelliously out of its braid and her shirtsleeves hiked up on her arms; nothing could induce her to spend the day in her bathrobe. And constantly she leapt to her feet on one pretext or another, while everybody cried, "Stop! Wait!" holding out their hands as if to catch the infant they imagined she would let drop.

Ian's father, who kept mostly to the basement these days, told Ian this was all a result of a misstep in evolution. "Human beings should never have risen upright," he said. "Now every pregnant woman has gravity working against her. Remember Claudia? Same thing happened to Claudia, back when she was expecting Franny."

"That's true, it did," Ian said. He had forgotten. All at once he saw Lucy in her red bandanna with her hair hanging down her back. "Just, you know, a little bleeding . . ." she informed him in her quaint croak. Lucy had been pregnant herself at the time. She had been pregnant at her wedding, most likely, and only now did Ian stop to think how she must have felt going through those early weeks alone, hiding her symptoms from everyone, trying to figure out some way to manage.

"It won't be real fancy," she said.

And, "Twenty twenty-seven! Great God Almighty!"

She said, "Do you think Danny will mind?"

That evening while he and Rita were playing Scrabble, he rose and wandered over to Lucy's framed photo above the piano. Daphne had hung it there some time ago, but he'd hardly glanced at it since. He lifted it from its hook and held it level in both hands. "I'll trade you two of my vowels for one consonant," Rita said, but Ian went on frowning at Lucy's small, bright face.

Of course, she struck him as preposterously young. That was

only to be expected. And everything about her was so dated. That leggy look of the sixties! That childish, Christopher Robin stance grown women used to affect, with their feet planted wide apart and their bare knees braced! She resembled a little tepee on stilts. A paper parasol from a cocktail glass. One of those tiny, peaked Japanese mushrooms with the thready stems.

He was noticing this to gain some distance. Surely he was able to see her clearly now. Wasn't he? Surely he had the perspective, at last, to understand what Lucy's meaning had been in his life.

But Rita said, "Okay, *three* of my vowels. For one lousy consonant. You drive a hard bargain, you devil."

And Ian replaced the picture on its hook, no wiser.

This was going to be the first Christmas of their marriage and Rita had big plans. She sent Daphne on mysterious errands with shopping lists and whispered instructions. She phoned Thomas in New York and Agatha in L.A., making sure they were coming. She drew up a guest list for Christmas dinner: Mrs. Jordan and the foreigners and her mother and Curt. Ian had once mentioned how the Bedloes' holiday meals used to be all hors d'oeuvres, and she decided to revive the practice even though it meant cooking from the living room. For days she lay on the couch with a breadboard across her lap, rolling pinwheels and stamping out fancy shapes of biscuit dough and mincing herbs that Doug obligingly toted back and forth for her. Ian worried she was overdoing, but at least it kept her entertained.

Christmas fell on a Monday that year. Thomas arrived in time for church on Sunday morning, and Daphne met them there, carrying her knapsack because she'd be sleeping over. Agatha and Stuart flew in that afternoon. For the family supper on Christmas Eve they had black-eyed peas and rice. Everybody was puzzled by this (they usually had oyster stew), but Rita explained that black-eyed peas were an ancient custom. Something to do with luck, she said—good luck for the coming year. Almost immediately a sort of click of recognition traveled around the table. Coming year? Then wasn't that *New Year's* Eve? They sent each other secret glances and then applied themselves to their food, smiling. Rita didn't notice a thing. Ian did, though, and he was touched by his family's tact. Lately he'd started valuing such qualities. He had begun to see the importance of manners and gracious gestures; he thought now that his mother's staunch sprightliness had been braver than he had appreciated in his youth. (Last summer, laid up for a week with a wrenched back, he had suddenly wondered how Bee had endured the chronic pain of her arthritis all those years. He suspected that had taken a good deal more strength than the brief, flashy acts of valor you see in the movies.)

"To the cook!" Thomas said, raising his water glass, and they all said, "To Rita!" Rita grinned and raised her own glass. Probably for decades of Christmas Eves to come the Bedloes would be loyally eating black-eyed peas and rice.

It was afterwards, in front of the fire, that Thomas announced his engagement. "You two won't be the newest newlyweds anymore," he told Ian. This wasn't exactly a shock—he'd been dating the same girl for some time now—but they had been hoping he would get over her. They all felt she bossed him around too much. (He kept falling for these managerial types who didn't have any softness to them; they might as well be business partners, Daphne had once complained.) Still, the women hugged him and Doug said, "What do you know!" and Ian suggested they call Angie and welcome her to the family. So they did, lining up in the hall to tell her more or less the same thing in several different ways. While Ian was waiting his turn at the phone he had a sudden memory of Danny presenting Lucy in this very spot. What was it he had said? "I'd like you to meet the woman who's changed my life," he had said, and then as now the family had received the news with the most resolute show of pleasure.

On Christmas morning they opened their presents—most of

Ian's and Rita's relating to babies—and then cleared away the gift wrap and started getting ready for the dinner guests. Rita directed from an armchair Ian had dragged into the dining room, except that she kept jumping up to do things herself. Finally Agatha put Stuart in charge of diverting her. "Show her your card tricks, Stu," she said. "Oh, please, no," Rita groaned. Ian and his father fitted all the leaves into the table, and the women added last-minute touches to the dishes Rita had prepared. Everyone was entranced to find nothing but hors d'oeuvres. "Look! Artichokes," Doug pointed out. "Look at this, kids, my favorite: Chesapeake crab spread. It's just like the old days." Rita beamed. Stuart told her, "Pick a card. Any card. Come on, Rita, pay attention."

The current foreigners' names were Manny, Mike, and Buck. They were the first to arrive—they always showed up on the dot, not familiar with Baltimore ways—and Mrs. Jordan followed, bearing one of her sumptuous black fruitcakes with the frosting you had to crack through with a chisel. Then Bobbeen appeared with an old-fashioned crank-style ice cream freezer, fully loaded and ready for the ice, and last came Curt, looking as if he'd just that minute rolled out of bed. Those who were guests had to have the hors d'oeuvres explained for them—all but Mrs. Jordan, of course, who'd been through this year after year. Mrs. Jordan said, "Why, you've even made Bee's hearts-of-palm dish!" And later, once they'd taken their seats and Doug had offered the blessing, she said, "Rita, if Ian's mother could see what you've done here she would be so pleased."

"Remember the first time we tasted hearts of palm?" Agatha asked Thomas.

"Was that when we had the flu?"

"No, no, this was before. You were really little, and Daphne was just a baby. I don't think she got to try them. But you and I were crazy about them; we polished off the platter. It wasn't till five or six years later we had that flu."

"Ugh! Worst flu of my life," Thomas said.

"Mine too. I couldn't eat a bite for days. But finally I called out, 'Ian, I'm hungry!' Remember, Ian? You were flat on your back—"

"*I* was sick?" Ian asked.

"Everyone was, even Grandma and Grandpa. You said, 'Hungry for what?' And I thought and thought, and the only thing that came to me was hearts of palm."

"So then we all wanted hearts of palm," Thomas told him. "They just sounded so *good*, even though I'd forgotten them and Daphne'd never had them. We said, 'Please, Ian, won't you please bring us hearts of—' "

"I don't remember this," Ian said.

"So you got up and tottered downstairs, holding onto the banister—"

"Put your coat on over your pajamas, stepped into somebody's boots—"

"Drove all the way to the grocery store and brought back hearts of palm."

"I don't remember any of it," Ian said.

They regarded him fondly—all but the foreigners, who were giving the hors d'oeuvres their single-minded attention. "My hero!" Rita told him.

"I said, 'Ian, thank you,' " Agatha went on, "and you said, 'Thank *you*. Until you mentioned them,' you said, 'I didn't realize that's what I'd been wanting all along myself.' "

Stuart said, "Maybe they contained some trace element your bodies knew they needed."

"Well, whatever," Curt said, "these here taste mighty good. You should go into the catering business, Rita."

"Oh, I believe I've got enough to do for the next little bit," she told him. And she patted her abdomen, which Ian's borrowed shirt could barely cover.

Daphne said, "Have you heard? After this baby's born, Rita and I are planning to be partners. Half the time I'll do clutter counseling while she stays home with the baby, half the time I'll stay with the baby while *she* does clutter counseling."

Ian raised his eyebrows. He knew Rita had been considering

various strategies, but she hadn't mentioned Daphne. He said, "What about Trips Unlimited?"

"That's not really working out," Daphne told him. "It's too personal."

"A travel agency is personal?"

"Mr. X and Mrs. Y book two flights to Paris and one hotel room, say, and I can't let on I've noticed. Or they cheat on their expense accounts with first-class reservations to—"

No one suggested that this new job would surely be even more personal—that she seemed to *search out* the personal. Finally Curt said, "Well, if you ever get tired of clutter counseling you could always become a scribe."

"Scribe?" Daphne asked, perking up.

"You could rent a stall at Harborplace and offer to write people's letters for them."

Daphne looked perplexed. The only person who laughed was Ian.

There was a little wait before dessert because they had to freeze the ice cream. Bobbeen said, "You realize we don't have a single child here? No one begging to turn the crank for us." But the foreigners, it emerged, would love to turn the crank. They rushed off to the kitchen while Daphne and Agatha cleared the table. Rita stayed seated at Ian's left, debating baby names with Mrs. Jordan. Curt was attempting to break into the fruitcake, and Thomas was telling his grandfather about his latest computer game. The idea was, he said, to show how dislodging one historical event could dislodge a hundred others, even those that seemed unrelated. "Take slavery," he said. "Students would tell the computer that the U.S. has never had slavery, and then they would name some later event. The computer goes, 'Beep!' and a message flashes up on the screen: *Null and void.*"

"But why would that be any fun?" Doug asked.

"Well, it's not supposed to be fun so much as educational."

"I wonder whatever became of Monopoly," Doug said wistfully.

Rita took Ian's hand and placed it palm-down on a spot just beneath her left breast. "Feel," she whispered. A round, blunt knob—a knee or foot or elbow—slid beneath his fingers. It always unnerved him when that happened.

Last week he had signed the papers for Rita's hospital stay. She'd be in just overnight, if everything went as it should. On the first day he was liable for one dependent and on the second, for two. Two? Then he realized: the baby. One person checks in; two check out. It seemed like sleight of hand. He had never noticed before what a truly astonishing arrangement this was.

"So I took a shortcut through a side street," Daphne told him, "or really more of an alley, and it was starting to get dark and I heard these footsteps coming up behind me. Pad-pad, pad-pad: gym-shoe footsteps. Rubber soles. I started walking faster. The footsteps walked faster too. I dug my hand in my bag and pulled out that siren you gave me. Remember that key chain with the siren on it you gave me one Christmas?"

They were heading down to the shop together to bring home the cradle. Ian was driving Rita's pickup, which had a balky gear shift that was annoying him no end. When the light turned green he had to struggle to get it into first. He said, "Very smart, Daphne. How many times have I warned you not to walk alone at night?"

"I spun around and I pressed the button. The siren went *wow! wow! wow!* and this person just about fell on top of me—this young, stalky black boy wearing great huge enormous white basketball shoes. He was shocked, you could tell. He backed off and sort of goggled at me. He said, 'What the hell, man? You know? What the hell?' And I was standing in front of him with my mouth wide open because I realized I had no idea how to switch the fool thing off. There we were, just looking at each other, and the siren going *wow! wow!* until bit by bit I started giggling. And then finally he kind of like shook his head and stepped around me. So I threw the siren over a fence and walked on, only making sure not to follow him too closely, and way far behind I could still hear *wow, wow, wow* . . ."

"You think it's all a big joke, don't you," Ian said, turning down Chalmer.

"Well, it was, in a way. I mean I wouldn't have been surprised if that boy had said, 'Oh, man, that uncle of yours,' while he was shaking his head. Like we were the old ones and you were the young one. You were the greenhorn."

"At least I won't end up dead in some alley," Ian told her. "What were you doing in that part of town? How come you're always cruising strange neighborhoods?"

"I like newness," Daphne said.

He parked in front of the wood shop.

"I like for things not to be too familiar. I like to go on first dates; I like it when a guy takes me someplace I've never been before, some restaurant or bar, and the waitress calls him by name and the bartender kids him but I'm the stranger, just looking around all interested at this whole new world that's so unknown and untried."

They got out of the truck. (Ian didn't ask how come she still lived in Baltimore, in that case. He was very happy she lived in Baltimore.) He walked around to the rear end to lower the tailgate, and he reached in for the folded blanket he'd brought and spread it across the floorboards.

"If I were a man I'd call up a different woman every night," Daphne said, following him. "I'd like that little thrill of not knowing if she would go out with me."

"Easy for *you* to say," Ian told her.

He didn't have to use his key to get into the shop, which meant Mr. Brant must be working on a weekend again. He ushered Daphne inside and led the way across the dusty linoleum floor, passing a half-assembled desk and the carcass of an armoire. Through the office doorway he glimpsed Mr. Brant bending over the drafting table, and he stepped extra heavily so as to make his presence felt. Mr. Brant raised his head but merely nodded, deadpan.

When they reached the corner that was Ian's work space, he came to a stop. He gestured toward the cradle—straight-edged and shining. "Well?" he said. "What do you think?"

"Oh, Ian, it's beautiful! Rita's going to love it."

"Well, I hope so," he said. He bent to lift it. The honey smell of Wood-Witch paste wax drifted toward him. "You take the other end. Be careful getting it past that desk; I spent a long time on the finish."

They started back through the shop, bearing the cradle between them. Mr. Brant came to the office doorway to watch, but Daphne didn't even glance in his direction. She was still talking about newness. "I'd call some woman I'd just seen across a room or something," she said. "I would *not* say, 'You don't know me, but—' That's such an obvious remark. Why would she need to be informed she doesn't know you, for goodness' sake?"

All at once it seemed time slipped, or jerked, or fell away beneath Ian's feet. He was fifteen years old and he was rehearsing to ask Cicely Brown to the Freshman Dance. Over and over again he dialed the special number that made his own telephone ring, and Danny picked up the receiver in the kitchen and pretended to be Cicely's mother. "*Yell*-ow," he answered in fulsome, golden tones, and then he'd call, "Cicely, dahling!" and switch to his Cicely voice, squeaky and mincing and cracked across the high notes. "Hello? Oooh! Ian-baby!" By that stage Ian was usually helpless with laughter. But Danny waited tolerantly, and then he led Ian through each step of the conversation. He told Ian it was good to hear from him. He asked how he'd done on the history test. He spent several minutes on the he-said-she-said girls always seemed to think was so important, although in this case it was, "He said mumble-grumble and she said yattata-yattata." Then he left a conspicuous space for Ian to state his business, after which he told him, why, of course; you bet; he'd be thrilled to go to the dance.

Daphne said, "Ian?"

He balanced his end of the cradle on one knee and turned away, blotting his eyes with his jacket sleeve. When he turned back he found Mr. Brant next to him. "Hot," Ian explained. It was January, and cold enough in the shop to see your breath, but Mr. Brant nodded as if he knew all about it and opened the front door for him. Ian and Daphne carried the cradle on out.

Rita started labor in the middle of a working day. Envisioning this moment earlier, Ian had expected it to be nighttime—Rita nudging him awake the way women did on TV—but it was a sunny afternoon in late February when Doreen came to the office door and said, "Ian! Rita's on the phone." The other men glanced up. "Sure you don't want to change your mind, now," one said, grinning. They'd acted much less guarded around him since the news of the baby.

On the phone Rita said she was fine, pains coming every five minutes, no reason to leave the shop yet unless he wanted. By the time he reached home, though (for of course he came immediately), things had speeded up and she said maybe they should think about getting to the hospital. She was striding back and forth in the living room, wearing her usual outfit of leather boots and maternity jeans and one of his chambray shirts. His father paced alongside her, all but wringing his hands. "I've *never* liked this stage, never liked it," he told Ian. "Shouldn't we make her sit down?"

"I'm more comfortable walking," Rita said.

For the last two weeks she had been allowed on her feet again, and Ian often felt she was making up for lost time.

It was the mildest February ever recorded—not even cool enough for a sweater—and Rita looked surprised when Ian wanted to bring her coat to the hospital. "You don't know what the weather will be like when you come home," he told her.

She said, "Ian. I'm coming home *tomorrow*."

"Oh, yes."

He seemed to be preparing for a moment far in the future. It was unthinkable that in twenty-four hours they'd be back in this house with a child.

At the hospital they whisked her away while he dealt with Admissions, and by the time they allowed him in the labor room she had turned into a patient. She lay in bed in a coarse white gown, her forehead beaded with sweat. Every two minutes or so her face seemed to flatten. "Are you all right?" he kept asking. "Should I be doing anything?"

"I'm fine," she said. Her lips were so dry they looked gathered. The nurse had instructed him to feed her chips of ice from a plastic bowl on the nightstand, but when he offered her one she turned her head away fretfully.

She used to seem so invulnerable. That may have been why he had married her. He had seen her as someone who couldn't be harmed, once upon a time.

It was dark before they wheeled her to the delivery room. The windowpanes flashed black as Ian walked down the hall beside her stretcher. The delivery room was a chamber of horrors— glaring white light and gleaming tongs and monstrous chrome machines. "You stand by her head, daddy," the doctor told him. "Hold onto mommy's hand." Somehow Rita found it in her to snicker at this, but Ian obeyed grimly, too frightened even to smile. Her hand was damp, and she squeezed his fingers until he felt his bones realigning.

"Any moment now," the doctor announced. Any moment what? Ian kept forgetting their purpose here. He was strained tight, like guitar strings, and all his stomach muscles ached from urging Rita to push. Couldn't women die of this? Yes, certainly they could die. It happened every day. He didn't see what prevented her from simply splitting apart.

"A fine boy," the doctor said, and he held up a slippery, angry, squalling creature trailing coils of telephone cord.

Ian released the breath that must have been trapped in his

chest for whole minutes. "It's over, sweetheart," he told Rita.
He had to raise his voice to be heard above the racket.

The doctor laid the baby in Rita's outstretched arms and she
hugged it to her, cupping its wet black head in one hand. "Hello,
Joshua," she said. She seemed to be smiling and weeping both.
The baby went on wailing miserably. "So, do you like him?" she
said, looking up at Ian.

"Of course," he told her.

It wrenched him that she'd felt the need to ask.

Eventually the baby was carted off somewhere, and Rita sent
Ian to make phone calls. In the waiting room he shook quarters
from the envelope she had prepared weeks earlier. He called each
of the numbers she'd written across the front—first Bobbeen, and
then his father, and then Daphne, Thomas, and Stuart (Agatha
was still at work), and Rita's two best friends. They all sounded
thrilled and amazed, as if they hadn't understood till now that
an actual baby would come of this. Bobbeen wanted to drive
right over. Ian persuaded her to wait, though. "You can visit her
tomorrow," he said. "But stop by early. They're letting her go
home right after lunch."

"Modern times!" Bobbeen marveled. "When Rita was born
I had to stay a week, and they didn't let Vic in the delivery room,
either. You-all are lucky."

It was on Rita's account that he'd asked Bobbeen to wait till
morning; he assumed she would be exhausted. But when he went
to her room he found her sitting upright, looking ready to spring
out of bed. Her hair was combed and she wore her flannel pajamas
in place of the hospital gown. "Eight pounds, four and a half
ounces," she said. She must be talking about the baby, who
wasn't there yet. They kept them in the nursery for the first few
hours. "He's got your mouth: those little turns at the corners.
And my dad's Italian hair. Oh, I *wish* they'd bring him in."

"Ah, well, you'll have him for the next eighteen years," Ian
said.

Eighteen years; merciful heavens.

He sat with her a while, listening to her rattle on, and then he kissed her good night. When he left, she was dialing her mother on the phone.

At home, a single lamp lit the front hall. His father must have gone to bed. It was after ten o'clock, Ian was amazed to see. He trudged up the stairs to his room.

Already Rita's pregnancy seemed so long ago. The pillow laid vertically to ease her backache, the opened copy of *Nine Months Made Easy*, and Doug's pocket watch, borrowed for its second hand—they struck him as faintly pathetic, like souvenirs of some old infatuation.

He sat on the bed to take off his shoes. Then he realized he would never manage to sleep. He was tired, all right, but keyed up. Padding softly in his socks, he went back downstairs to the kitchen and switched on the light. He poured milk into a saucepan and lit a burner, and while he waited for the milk to heat he dialed Reverend Emmett.

"Hello," Reverend Emmett said, sounding wide awake.

"Reverend Emmett, this is Ian. I hope you weren't in bed."

"Goodness, no. What's the news?"

"Well, we have a boy. Joshua. Eight pounds and some."

"Congratulations! How's Sister Rita?"

"She's fine," Ian told him. "It was a very easy birth, she says. To me it didn't look easy, but—"

"Shall I go visit her tomorrow?"

"They're sending her home in the afternoon. Maybe you'd like to come see her here."

"Gladly," Reverend Emmett said. "Why, we haven't had a new baby at church since Sister Myra's granddaughter! I may have forgotten how to hold one."

"You're welcome to brush up on your skills with us," Ian told him.

"God bless you for thinking to call me, Brother Ian," Reverend Emmett said. "I know absolutely that you'll be a good father. Go get some rest now."

"I believe I will," Ian said.

In fact, all at once he felt so sleepy that after he hung up, he turned off the stove and went straight to bed.

He stepped out of his shirt and his jeans and lay down in his underwear, not even bothering to pull the covers over him. He closed his eyes and saw Rita's glowing face and the baby's expression of outrage. He saw Reverend Emmett attempting to hold an infant. *That* would be a sight. It intrigued him to imagine the incongruity—to try and picture Reverend Emmett in this new context, the way he used to try picturing his seventh-grade teacher doing something so mundane as cooking breakfast for her husband.

Apparently, he thought, there were people in this world who simply never came clear. Reverend Emmett, Mr. Brant, the overlapping shifts of foreigners . . . In the end you had to accept that the day would never arrive when you finally understood what they were all about.

For some reason, this made him supremely happy. He pulled the covers around him and said a prayer of thanksgiving and fell headlong into sleep.

"This is proper gift," the foreigner named Buck told Ian. Or Ian *thought* he told him; then a moment later he realized it must have been a question. "This is proper gift?"

He meant the white plastic potty-chair resembling a real toilet, a pink ribbon tied in a bow across the seat like one of those hygienic paper bands in hotel bathrooms. Buck and Manny held it balanced between them on the top porch step. If Ian answered, "No," they seemed ready to spin around and take it home with them. He said, "Of course it's proper. Thank you very much."

"In America, every what you do is proper," Manny said to Buck. They appeared to be resuming some previous argument. "Why you are always so affrighted?"

"Wrong," Buck said. "They *tell* you is proper. Then catch

your mistake. Ha!" he cried, startling Ian. "Pink ribbon. For boys should be blue."

"We already have been discussing this," Manny told him severely. "It is no problem." He turned to Ian. "Pink or blue: is all the same to you. Correct?"

"Correct," Ian assured him. "Come on inside."

He stood back, holding open the door, and they carried the potty through the front hall and into the living room. Rita sat in the rocker with a large pillow beneath her. Daphne and Reverend Emmett shared the couch. "This is proper gift," Buck told them. He and Manny set the potty on the floor.

"Well, certainly," Rita said, "and it's exactly what we wanted. Thank you, Buck and Manny."

"Is also from Mike. Mike has been arrested."

"Arrested?"

But before they could get to the bottom of this, Bobbeen called, "Yoo-hoo!" and let herself in. Her heels clattered across the hall and then she appeared in the doorway, wearing an orange pantsuit with a flurry of silk scarf tied artfully at her throat. She held both arms out at her sides; a vinyl purse dangled from one wrist. "Well?" she said. "Where is he? Where'd you put him? Where's that precious little grandbaby?"

"Hi, Ma," Rita said. "You remember Buck and Manny here, and Reverend Emmett."

"Oh! Goodness *yes*, I do," Bobbeen said, directing her squinty grimace solely to Reverend Emmett. He was standing now, look- ing uncomfortable, and Bobbeen stepped forward to grasp his hands in hers. "Wasn't it Christian of you to take this time from your duties," she said. Ian always suspected her of harboring a romantic interest in Reverend Emmett, but maybe she was just exceptionally devout. "Hey there, Daphne hon," she added over her shoulder. She sat in the center of the couch, pulling Reverend Emmett down beside her. "I can't believe I'm a grandma," she told him. "Isn't it a hoot? I sure don't *feel* like a grandma."

She didn't look like one either, Reverend Emmett was supposed to say, but he just smiled hard and clutched both his kneecaps. Bobbeen studied him a moment. She patted the ends of her hair reflectively and then turned to Rita. "So where's that little sweetie pie?" she asked.

"Ian was just on his way to bring him down," Rita told her.

He was?

Before the foreigners arrived, Reverend Emmett and Daphne had been about to follow him upstairs and peek into the cradle. But now there were too many of them, Ian supposed, and so he nodded and left the room. He was a little out of practice, was the trouble. He wasn't sure he remembered how to support a newborn's head.

As he started up the stairs he heard Bobbeen say, "Now tell me, Reverend Emmett, do you-all hold with christening? Or just what, exactly?"

"We believe christening to be a superficial convention," Reverend Emmett said.

"Well, of *course* it is," she told him in a soothing tone.

"Not to say there's anything wrong with it, you understand. It's just that we don't consider infants capable of . . . but if *your* church favors christening, why, I certainly—"

"Oh, what do I care about christening?" Bobbeen cried recklessly. "I think it's real holy of you to cast off the superficial, Reverend."

Ian went into his and Rita's bedroom, where they were keeping the baby for the first few nights. It lay facedown in one corner of the cradle with its knees drawn up to its stomach and its nose pressed into the sheet. How could it manage to breathe that way? But Ian heard tiny sighing sounds. Long strands of fine black hair wisped past the neckband of the flannel gown. Ian felt a surge of pity for those scrawny, hunched, defenseless little shoulders.

He knelt beside the cradle and turned the baby over, at the same time gingerly scooping it up so that he held a warm, wrinkled bundle against his chest as he rose. This didn't feel like any eight pounds. It felt like nothing, like thistledown—a burden so light it seemed almost buoyant; or maybe he was misled by the softness of the flannel. The baby stirred and clutched two minia- ture handfuls of air but went on sleeping. Ian bore his son gently across the upstairs hall.

"In fact I've been thinking of joining your congregation," Bobbeen was telling Reverend Emmett. "Did Rita happen to mention that?"

"Um, no, she didn't."

"I just feel you-all might have the answers."

"Oh, well, *answers*," Reverend Emmett said. "Actually, Mrs.—"

"Bobbeen."

"Actually, Mrs. Bobbeen . . ."

Ian grinned.

He was halfway down the stairs when he felt a kind of echo effect—a memory just beyond his reach. He paused, and Danny stepped forward to present his firstborn. "Here she is!" he said. But then the moment slid sideways like a phonograph needle skipping a groove, and all at once it was Lucy he was presenting. "I'd like you to meet the woman who's changed my life," he said. His face was very solemn but Lucy was smiling. "Your what?" she seemed to be saying. "Your, what was that? Oh, your *life*." And she tipped her head and smiled. After all, she might have said, this was an ordinary occurrence. People changed other people's lives every day of the year. There was no call to make such a fuss about it.

A NOTE ABOUT THE AUTHOR

Anne Tyler was born in Minneapolis, Minnesota, in 1941 but grew up in Raleigh, North Carolina. She graduated at nineteen from Duke University, and went on to do graduate work in Russian studies at Columbia University. This is Anne Tyler's twelfth novel; her last novel, *Breathing Lessons*, was awarded the Pulitzer Prize in 1988. She is a member of the American Academy and Institute of Arts and Letters. She and her husband, Taghi Modarressi, live in Baltimore, Maryland.